A Rachel Markham Mystery

MURDER

AT RUTHERFORD HALL

D1383628

notionpress.com

About Notion Press

Notion Press is a Self-publishing platform to write, publish & sell Print books and eBook around the world. To learn more, visit www.notionpress.com

Murder At Rutherford Hall is product of the Notion Press Author Incubation Program.

A Rachel Markham Mystery

MURDER
AT RUTHERFORD HALL

P.B. KOLLERI

notionpress.com

First published by NotionPress 2013

ISBN: 9781481977876

Dedicated to our beloved Agatha Christie

For gifting us hours of reading pleasure

Chapter One

ENGLAND. NOVEMBER 1946.

It was half past seven on a November evening. A thick fog had descended on the English countryside. A lone set of headlights could be seen making their way on a narrow winding road on this dark foggy evening. Jeremy Richards, the man driving the car, was what most people would call a good looking man in an 'uncut diamond' sort of way. He had an easy manner, almost casual. Even in a formal dinner jacket, which he had on under his grey coat, he looked as comfortable as a farm hand. He wore his clothes carelessly as if he didn't really care about his appearance. Most people would say that he looked quite young for his age – about 35 when he had really turned 42 this past summer. A tall man, he stood six feet two inches in his socks, had an aquiline nose, a determined jaw and deep set brown eyes that shone with intelligence and humour under normal circumstances and had quite the melting effect on the opposite sex. However, today was not one of those days.

The weather had been depressingly grey and cold through the past few days and now as he drove the car, it seemed to Jeremy that the fog was thicker close to the ground which made driving down these narrow winding English country roads that much more difficult. *'Confounded fog... can't see a thing! Wish I was home in front of the log fire instead of traipsing around the countryside in this blasted weather!'* Jeremy cursed inwardly as he drove his new 1945 MG Midget at a snail's pace. Even as he peered through his windscreen, he felt one tire go over something like a large stone. *'Damn and blast! Maybe I should just turn the car around and go right back home.'* But then he knew he was almost there and besides if he tried to turn the car, he was liable to end up reversing into a ditch. His destination: Rutherford Hall, three miles away from his own country cottage in the village. The occasion: An invitation for cocktails and dinner by his neighbours Lord and Lady Charles Rutherford. As the Rutherford culinary spread and wine cellars were famous in this part of the country, for their sheer excellence, Jeremy pacified himself. Dinner would probably be an excellent meal and he could relax once he reached the hall. 'Hope it's worth the bloody drive...' he muttered to himself.

He had met Lord Charles Rutherford a week ago, at the Church fete, where Lord Rutherford had been asked to cut the ribbon and give the usual speech. He had liked the man. About 55, he seemed like an interesting person with a bluff sense of humour and frank blue eyes. They had got talking and Rutherford had invited him over for this dinner party. Other than that one brief meeting, Jeremy knew very little about his neighbours. But he had been living in a self-created isolation for long enough and decided it was time he started getting about and moved on with his life.

So here he was, driving towards Rutherford Hall on this gloomy Friday night. And it felt like the drive was taking forever. On the next turn, he heaved a sigh of relief. The massive wrought iron gates, flanked by 2 enormous pillars with gargoyles seated on them, became dimly visible on the right. One of the two large gates was open and he gingerly manoeuvred the MG Midget through the open half of the gate. He picked up the pace a bit on the driveway to the hall. The drive to the hall by itself would have been a beautiful one on a golden summer afternoon, as it was flanked on either side by cedar trees and then woodlands and acres of rolling parklands that made the estate a tourist magnet all through summer. But on an evening like this with close to zero visibility, the beauty of it all lay hidden behind a curtain of deep gloomy fog.

He drove for what seemed about half a mile and then suddenly, without warning, like an apparition out of thin air, he saw a woman in an ivory satin evening gown, with blond hair flying, running towards the car. She was looking over her shoulder into the darkness and running as if she was fleeing from a terrifying pursuer. She whipped her head around as the headlights fell on her, and Jeremy got a glimpse of wide-eyed terror. He hit the brakes and swerved wildly, but it was too late to prevent the collision. He heard a scream and then a dull thud and all was quiet. It all happened in seconds. *Oh my God!*

He got out and saw the woman's body huddled in a heap in front of the headlights, with her hands held up in front of her body in an instinctive shield. There was blood on her hands and on her ivory satin evening dress. She was completely unconscious. He got on his knees and cradled her head on his lap. Quickly moving her heavy pearl choker and jewelled beads aside, and reached for the carotid artery in her neck. There was a faint but steady pulse. *Thank God she's alive. Please don't let her die on me!* He lifted her body in his arms, and though she looked as slim as a waif, her body felt like dead weight. Lifting her, he started walking as quickly as he could, trying not to panic, towards the house. He heard footsteps running on the gravel path. He wondered if those were the footsteps she was running from. They seemed to be coming towards him, but he couldn't be sure. "Over here! Help me. There's been an accident," he yelled out through the fog.

A few more steps and Jeremy could now hear the faint sounds of a party tinkling somewhere just ahead, and then the lights of the house came into view. And a man's silhouette became visible as a flashlight shone out of the fog.

"Are you alright Sir? We heard a scream. I'm Hopworth, the butler," the man said as he walked towards him. Jeremy's professional eye quickly assessed that the man was about5'7", with a portly build and a dignified gait. He knew instinctively that he was indeed who he claimed to be - the butler of Rutherford Hall.

"I'm alright. But this lady came running out of nowhere, and I'm afraid my car hit her. This terrible fog, you see. No, it's alright I'll manage carrying her into the house, if you could only show me the way. I need you to call in a doctor as soon as we get her inside the house. I fear she's been hurt rather badly. Do you know who she is?"

"Why, Sir! This is Lady Celia - the mistress of the Hall!" he said in a hushed tone.

II

Hopworth had left Jeremy in the library as Lady Celia was carried up to her room where the doctor could attend to her in peace once he arrived. Jeremy was relieved he didn't have to face the other guests just yet. He wondered what he would say to them or to the rest of the family. Hello! *It's nice to meet you. Ghastly weather this. And oh, by the way, I've just knocked down the hostess with my car.*

Then his mind went back to Lady Celia. She was probably one of the most beautiful women he had ever come across, and he had come across many through his work and otherwise. As he had carried her to the house, he had the chance to get a good look at her under the light in the hall and was taken aback at how perfect her features were. She had gorgeous curls of long honey blond hair coming down to her waist, the perfect nose, full bow shaped rose coloured lips and high cheek bones. And although he was no expert on women's make-up, he was quite sure the Lady Celia's blemish-free alabaster skin owed very little to artifice. Hers was a rare beauty that was purely natural, and somehow she reminded him of Ophelia in the play he had seen at the old Vic. He found himself thinking that Sir Charles Rutherford was a very lucky man indeed.

His reverie was cut short as the study door opened.

Elizabeth Markham walked in to the library, followed by Hopworth. She made quite a picture against the panelled oak and old masters. A tall stately woman dressed in a spectacular purple silk gown, she seemed to fit right in with the gilded surroundings. She had a regal bearing and an ageless look about her. She was one of those women who could be anywhere in her 30s to 50s. Jeremy Richards had been standing in front of the fire place looking into the flames, and he turned around to greet her. *Another beauty, but this one probably owes a great deal to artifice and hard work,* he thought, smiling inwardly – so different from the kind he had just encountered. This, on the other hand, was the perfect face to adorn a portrait of the Lady of the Manor. *I bet she never loses her self-control. Quite the coldblooded aristocrat.*

She looked at him and said, "Do sit down, Mr. Richards. We've telephoned Dr. James Devine, but his housekeeper informs us that he is already on his way to attend the party here tonight, so I'm sure he will be with us shortly. This is really quite strange. What was Celia running from, I wonder! And no one can locate Charles! Really! My brother can be so absent-minded. He's probably even forgotten he's invited all these people to dinner! Hopworth, please ask Gladys to send us a hot brandy and some refreshment for Mr. Richards."

"Yes, madam," Hopworth said as he retreated, closing the study doors behind him.

The doors reopened and a high spirited young woman in her early twenties, with shingled auburn hair, wearing a bright shimmering scarlet dress cut in the latest fashionable style, came into the study in a state of excitement. She addressed Elizabeth, "Oh Mummy, I've just heard! And to think I was just moaning to Dennis in the afternoon about how boring the country is and that nothing ever happens here!"

"Rachel dear, I don't believe you've met Mr. Jeremy Richards? Mr. Richards - this is my daughter Rachel."

"Oh hello! I didn't see you there. Isn't this a hoot! Straight out of those detective novels one reads for excitement. I say! Aren't you the Scotland Yard detective? Uncle Charles told me he met you and you had taken up a house in the village. My! News does travel fast. Bodies dropping everywhere all of a sudden, and here you are, already on the crime scene!" Rachel said, her words tumbling over each other.

"Sorry to disappoint you. I am no longer with Scotland Yard. Matter of fact, I took early retirement last year. Afraid, it was my car that caused all this trouble. Lady Celia just seemed to appear in front of it, and there was nothing I could do really. Luckily I was only going at about five miles an hour!" Jeremy said to her.

Lady Elizabeth cut in reassuringly, "Oh, I am quite sure it wasn't your fault Mr. Richards. There is a terrible fog out there tonight. And do behave yourself Rachel. I won't have you gloating on about excitement when your aunt has just been knocked down in this unfortunate car accident."

"Oh I am sorry Mums. Didn't mean to be heartless. It's just that nothing ever happens here, and all of a sudden there's just so much going on. And Celia isn't really my aunt, Mums. She's only about a year or two older than I am. Rather funny calling her Aunt Celia. Doing that would be heartless. Don't you agree, Mr. Richards?"

"Oh, ah well," stammered Jeremy, not knowing quite what to say.

Rachel looked point blank at Jeremy and said "Speaking of young...you look a bit young for a retired old fogey yourself, Mr. Richards. But you do look like a real detective though, the kind one reads about in books. Pity really that there's no gruesome murder mystery to solve here!"

"Really Rachel! That's quite enough. Can you please make yourself useful and go and ask your father and Dennis to join us in the library? They can probably make some excuse to the other dinner guests and put an end to this party," Lady Elizabeth told her.

"Oh! Daddy and Dennis are with Lydia in Celia's room. They carried her up. I just had a word with Lydia upstairs. She asked me to send the maids up. Lydia is Celia's mother, you know. She stays here," Rachel added by way of explanation to Jeremy. "It seems they're all mooning over her. Celia's quite the drama queen now that she's regained consciousness."

"Has she? May I see her then? I would like to apologize in person. Hope she's not too badly hurt," Jeremy said, hoping beyond hope that the blood he had seen was from a superficial wound.

"Well, they say there are no broken bones, if that helps. You probably could see her, but you see, she won't have a clue as to who you are. Thing is, Celia says *she can't remember what happened!*" Rachel replied.

"Can't remember?" Lady Elizabeth asked with a raised eyebrow.

"Not a thing apparently!" Rachel replied smugly.

"It is known to happen. Sometimes a concussion or a traumatic shock can cause temporary amnesia," Jeremy said.

"Oh! I do hope Dr. Devine gets here fast. Wonder what's taking him so long!" Elizabeth wondered out loud.

Chapter Two

Half an hour later, the nine odd dinner guests had left Rutherford Hall amidst much confusion and expressions of concern regarding the accident. James Markham, Lady Elizabeth's husband, had spoken on behalf of his brother-in-law, Sir Charles, to the room full of guests, expressing his profuse apologies as he announced that Lady Celia had just had a car accident, and in view of that, it would be better to give Sir Charles and Lady Celia some rest. Dr. James Devine had arrived by then and was escorted upstairs to Lady Celia's room.

A small group of people clustered at the foot of the stairs in the hall waiting for Dr. Devine to come down after examining Celia. Jeremy observed everyone. He looked at Dennis Hawthorne standing by Rachel's side and found himself wondering about him. *Where had he seen that face before*? He couldn't quite place the young man, but he was certain that the brooding eyes, wavy dark hair and Byronic features were familiar, and that he had seen him somewhere before, perhaps in a photograph. *Or was it in a case file at Scotland Yard?* It would eventually come to him. Rachel was saying something to him, in her usual animated way, but Dennis seemed too preoccupied to take notice. He was sure that Dennis Hawthorne was deeply immersed in his own world of thoughts, and blasé to the conversations flying around him.

Next to them, Lady Elizabeth was speaking quietly with her husband James Markham. She was concerned about not being able to locate her brother Charles yet. James Markham, on the other hand, had moved on to a more mundane topic of whether or not they ought to start the dinner service for the rest of the family. Then they looked up as they saw Dr. Devine coming down the stairs.

"So what's the verdict, Doctor?" Rachel asked him.

"Oh, she'll live. A few bad bruises. She's had a shock you know. I've given her a strong sedative and it is best she sleeps it off for now. We'll have to keep her under observation. Her mother is with her for now, but I'll ring the nursing home and ask for a nurse to attend to her for the next few days. But look here Markham - I want a private word with you," he said, drawing James Markham aside.

Then, in a hushed tone, he whispered to Markham, "There's something that concerns me more. There seem to be no major cuts anywhere on her, and yet her hands and dress were quite covered in blood. Human blood, to the best of my knowledge. Makes me wonder where it came from. Certainly not from her."

"What are you trying to say, old boy?" James Markham enquired, looking worried.

"I am saying that someone, somewhere has been hurt a lot worse, and unfortunately Celia doesn't remember where she was, or with whom she was, before she regained consciousness in her room."

"Good gracious! Must find Charles and tell him to gather his staff and start looking about on this estate. Someone could be hurt or worse!" James Markham exclaimed.

"I'm betting on worse. It may be a good idea to call the police now," was the Doctor's grim reply.

"It's a bit premature for that, don't you think, Doctor. We don't want to trouble the good old constabulary for nothing. For all you know, there could be a simple explanation for all this," said James and then he turned back and asked everyone in general, "Anyone managed to find Charles yet? Need to form a search party. We need to look for someone wounded and probably bleeding on the grounds. Someone Celia had encountered before she met with her car accident."

Lady Elizabeth spoke up as if coming out of a daze, "Oh my God. I do hope Charles is alright. He seems to have disappeared. No one has seen him over the past hour or so. Oh, James - do take the boys and ask Hopworth to get the staff together. We must find him. I'm really beginning to worry now!"

"Don't worry, old girl," James comforted her. "We don't know that its Charles yet, could be anyone. A tramp or someone from outside. Besides, Charles could have just taken a walk. We're likely to find him safe and sound, probably strolling around somewhere. Come on then, gentlemen. Mr. Richards, we'll need your help. You've probably got plenty of experience in this sort of thing."

"Oh, please call me Jeremy. And yes, I'd very much like to help. Let's get the search party organised," Jeremy said, taking control of the situation.

II

An hour later, the ladies were in the drawing room as Dennis Hawthorne walked in. He headed towards the marble table, on which a tray of port and glasses had been placed earlier. "No sign of Charles yet, I'm afraid," he said helping himself to a glass of port.

Elizabeth and Rachel were seated on the couch.

"Oh dear! That's awful. If he's hurt somewhere, he probably needs immediate medical attention," Elizabeth said, sounding concerned.

"I dare say, but can't imagine where he could have gotten to! We checked everywhere on the grounds around the house, the conservatory, the summer house, and I'm sure the staff have gone through every one of the 25 rooms in the house by now. Of course, the estate is extensive and if he's walked out to meet someone through the woods, he could be in the village by now," Dennis said.

"But why on earth would he go out to the village to meet someone when he invited all these people to dinner?" Elizabeth wondered out loud.

"You know how absent-minded he is, Mother. Besides, Uncle Charles does love to walk everywhere. He says it keeps him fit as a fiddle," Rachel said.

"Not in this weather, it wouldn't. He'll be more likely to catch his death with pneumonia! Not the kind of night that would tempt anyone to walk about for no reason. Perhaps he's taken the car," Elizabeth said, looking expectantly at Dennis.

"No chance of that. Hopworth spoke to the chauffeur, can't remember his name..." Dennis said, trying to think.

"Giles," Rachel prompted.

"Yes, Giles, and he says all cars are in the garage including Mr. Richard's car, which he moved from the driveway. So it looks like wherever your brother has gone, it's definitely on foot," Dennis explained.

"This is turning into a first class mystery! First Celia runs off and gets hit by a car, and now no one can find Uncle Charles! " Rachel spoke up.

"Oh and Major Markham asked me to inform you that he's rung the station and the police are going to file a missing persons report for now," Dennis added.

"Good. High time someone called the police!" Elizabeth said.

"The Sergeant said they would be here first thing in the morning to investigate further. Of course, we are to keep them informed, should the good Lord return home in the wee hours of the morn! He seems to think that a buxom wench may be involved... " Dennis added with a smile.

"Yes, that's enough, thank you Dennis. I don't really care about what that silly sergeant thinks. Wish you young people would stop being so flippant about everything in life!"

"I think it's terribly unfair to shoot the messenger, don't you Rachel?" Dennis asked with a pleasant smile.

"Aye Sir, I do!" Rachel said laughingly.

At that moment, Mrs. Lydia Holden, Celia's mother, walked into the drawing room. Lydia Holden looked tired. One could tell by looking at her that, in her youth, she must've been a pretty woman with sharp features and possibly golden hair. Now, there were lines on her face and the gold in her hair had turned a mousy blond with streaks of grey through it. She had a medium build, and there was nothing distinguishing about her features except for a sharp nose and a pair of what could be described as 'fine grey eyes.' Unfortunately, the years of hardship she had endured after her husband's death had left a shrewish expression in them, and a set of thin lips to match. She had a habit of looking at you with her head tilted to one side - a coquettish gesture in youth which took on a slightly theatrical effect on an older woman. She walked over and sat down heavily on the sofa, facing Dennis.

"How is Celia now?" Dennis asked her.

"She's fast asleep. I've just left her with the nurse Dr. Devine sent over from the nursing home. Extraordinary thing, her running out into the night like that. Girls! One never knows what's going on in their minds these days. She's always been such a secretive little thing. And where is that husband of hers, I'd like to know. Hasn't come in once to see her yet. Really, the things that go on in this house! " Lydia said, looking quite irritated.

"Haven't you heard? Uncle Charles is missing. Daddy has just called up the police to file a missing persons report," Rachel said to Lydia.

"Why I never! No one tells me anything! Elizabeth, is this true?" Lydia turned to ask her.

"Yes. Dr. Devine said that Celia had blood on her hands, and it wasn't hers, so we're all rather worried about it. It could be Charles'. The thing that bothers me is *not knowing* what's happened. We're as much in the dark as you. Did Celia say anything at all in the room?" Elizabeth asked Lydia.

"No, that's just it. That girl has never confided in me in the best of times, and today she just kept saying she can't remember. Can't remember anything, poppycock! I think she's afraid, and she's hiding something. Now Charles is missing. Oh God! I hope she's not gone and done anything awful," Lydia answered.

"I won't have you all talk about Celia like this!" Dennis said with anger and stood up. "How can you even think that about her? She's been in an accident that was bad enough to knock the living daylights out of anyone. So stop insinuating she had anything to do with whatever you think has happened to Charles... We don't even know what's happened. *And you, Lydia - how could you? When you know she's incapable of hurting a fly!*" And with that, he stalked out of the room.

Rachel jumped up and followed him out. "Dennis, wait! Wait for me."

Chapter Three

"Dennis, wait up!" Rachel said, running behind him.

"Just leave me alone...all of you!" he shouted, striding off.

"But Dennis...that's just it. You ought not to be left alone at a time like this. Look here, Dennis!" she said, reaching out to touch his shoulder. He turned towards her. "You have to be reasonable. Mums and Lydia are just upset. You know they're fond of Celia. Lydia is her mother! Thing is, no one knows what's going on, and the only person who might have some idea is Celia and she's not talking," she said in a quiet voice.

"So you all jump to the conclusion that she's to blame somehow for a crime that *may or may not* have been committed," he shouted.

"There was all that blood on her hands, Dennis. It's only natural to think Celia ought to know how it got on her hands in the first place," she said, raising her voice.

"Celia! Celia! Celia! I am fed up to my teeth with all of you trying to hang her already. God! I need a stiff drink," he said, suddenly looking depressed.

"There's some whiskey in the library. I know Uncle Charles keeps it in one of the writing bureaus."

"Fine. Let's go there. If you want to keep me company, you had better join me for a drink, Rachel."

"I don't know. Don't think Mums would be too pleased if she found me drinking at this time of night. Left to her, I'd be up in bed by now!" Rachel replied, grimacing.

"What is it about you girls and your mother fixation? Mother won't like this. Mother won't like that! It's like you don't have a mind of your own. How old are you?"

"I'm twenty-three, and I don't have a mother fixation. You men are different. So independent. I do envy your freedom sometimes."

"I don't believe it for a minute. You sound positively Victorian. It's 1946! Women have complete freedom to do as they please these days. Seems to me, you women always manage to do exactly what you want to do, and when you don't want to do something, you just make an excuse and blame it on Mother!"

"That's not true!"

"Really?"

"Well, it may be true to some extent...come to think of it. Alright, I'll join you for that drink."

"Atta girl!"

The library was in darkness as the fire in the fireplace had died down, but the door was open as they walked in.

"I like you, Dennis. Really, I do. You make me think." Rachel said.

"And what have I made you think of now?"Dennis asked her.

"That you are very much in love with Celia," she said looking at him meaningfully.

"Is it that obvious?" he said, raising his voice, as if he was angry with himself.

"Frankly, yes!" she said, in a raised voice to match his, as she walked towards the writing bureau and switched on the green banker's lamp on the desk.

That's when they noticed Jeremy Richards in the library, sitting with his eyes closed in one of the armchairs. As they turned to look at him, wondering how much of their conversation he may have overheard, Jeremy slowly opened his eyes and smiled, "You've caught me napping."

"Sorry, we didn't mean to disturb your forty winks, Mr. Richards. Do you mind terribly if we hunt around for some whiskey. Dennis wants a stiff one," Rachel said with a grin.

"Not at all. Wouldn't mind having one myself," Jeremy replied.

Rachel walked over to the corner bureau, opened it, and brought out a bottle of Vintage Scottish Single Malt. "I'm sure Uncle Charles wouldn't mind. After all, he is responsible for our sleepless night!" she said, handing it to Dennis. "And look, there are exactly three glasses here. Dennis, would you like to do the honours?"

Dennis poured out a good measure into the glasses and handed them around.

"To your Uncle Charles. May he be found," Dennis said, as he took a gulp.

"I do hope he's alright," Rachel said. *"Don't know if not finding him* is good news or bad."

"I'll admit, it's perplexing. A well-known man like that simply disappearing into thin air. Perhaps Lady Celia will be able to throw some light on the matter in the morning," Jeremy said, taking a sip of the whiskey.

"Oh, Mr. Richards. Don't start Dennis up again. He's already upset with Mums and Lydia because they thought that she had something to do with Uncle Charles disappearing."

"She has nothing to do with it, I tell you! At the most, she witnessed something and went into a state of shock. Celia wouldn't hurt a fly. She's the gentlest girl I know. None of you *really know* her the way I do," Dennis said, lighting up a cigarette.

"You've known her since she was a little girl, haven't you?" Rachel asked.

"Yes. Back in India..." Dennis said, settling down comfortably into an old leather armchair. He inhaled deeply and blew out a smoke ring. "Her father Augustus Holden and mine both managed neighbouring tea estates for the Darjeeling Consolidated Tea Company in Bengal. Have you ever seen a tea estate?" he asked, looking at Rachel.

"No. Can't say that I have. Besides, I've never been to India. What's it like?" Rachel queried.

"Oh Rachel, it's like a piece of heaven. Or what I'd imagine heaven to be, I suppose." Then looking abstractedly through the window he continued, "The tea plantations are all up in the hills near the foothills of the majestic Himalayas – the greatest mountain range in the world. Nothing can quite prepare you for the first time you catch a glimpse of the Himalayas – the ice mountains. Takes your breath away. It is indescribably beautiful. Our tea estates were up near the hills in Bengal, from where you could see the ice peaks at a distance. And when you stood on one of these estates you felt you were surrounded by undulating shades of green – for acres and acres, like a carpet made up of every shade of green known to man. I have never felt such a sense of tranquillity anywhere else. Makes you see that all's right with the world. Celia and I would sit together quietly for hours and just watch the clouds play shadow and light games with the carpet of green for as far as the eye could see and then the ice mountains beyond. I can still see it so clearly. The native tea pickers singing a rhythmic song as they went about picking the tender tea leaves just after sunrise. The morning mist thinning out and then disappearing down into the valley. The colours are like nothing you can see over here. Everything is so muted here. There's nothing mute about India. Even the flowers blaze at you. The native hill people are wonderful. So simple and childlike. I've seen grown men cry loudly like children when they are unhappy and when they are happy, their laughter is so real, like a child's laughter. Makes your heart want to sing out with joy." Then as if coming out of a trance, he took another sip. "Why are you looking at me so strangely?" he asked them both.

"It could be that I've never seen this side to you, Dennis. Hearing you speak about India is just so lyrical. So lovely, like a poem. Isn't it, Mr. Richards?" Rachel asked.

"I agree. You ought to be a writer Mr. Hawthorne," Jeremy added.

"Oh, but he is, Mr. Richards and quite a famous one at that. His first book just got published and it's simply flying off the shelves, isn't it Dennis?" Rachel said, her eyes lighting up.

"Ha! One measly book and a bunch of newspaper reviews does not make one a famous author by a long shot, my dear girl!" Dennis responded modestly.

"Ah! Now I remember! That's where I saw your picture. In the Times about a month ago. An article on young, upcoming English authors. I knew there was something familiar about your face. Forgive me for not having read your book, but I've been pretty out of it all in the recent months...burying myself in the country. Trying to get away from it all," Jeremy said, with a sardonic smile.

"Did Scotland Yard get too hectic for you?" Rachel asked.

"My dear young lady, my entire life has been too hectic for me. Thought I'd never manage to tear myself away after years of trying to flee the bustling beehive. I dislike London - always have. Too many people. Never felt quite at home as I do here," Jeremy said with a smile.

"I envy you, Mr. Richards. No place feels like home to me anymore," Dennis said with a sad look and continued.

"No, I'd give anything to be back in India given half a chance. The only place where I could breathe again. I daresay, I've coloured my childhood memories a bit. And seeing Celia again reminded me once more...if only things were different...I can't help thinking of what might have been."

"You mean if Celia hadn't married my Uncle Charles?" Rachel asked.

"Yes," Dennis said simply.

"Why didn't you marry her when you had the chance Dennis?" Rachel asked.

"It's a long story and a boring one. I'm not sure I want to bore either of you to death yet," Dennis replied.

"Oh, I'm willing to take the risk if you are, Mr. Richards. It's not like we're going anywhere for the time being anyway," Rachel said with an impish smile.

"By all means. We all have to die sometime you know!" Jeremy said with a wink in Rachel's direction, and then looking at Dennis said, "No, really. All jokes aside, I'd be most interested to hear about your life in India."

"Oh do tell us more! What was Celia like? I mean as a child. How old was she when you first met her?" Rachel asked Dennis.

Dennis smiled and said, "Let me see. Yes. I met Celia for the first time when I had come back from boarding school to spend the summer with my folks in India. She must've been ten years old. I remember she showed me her little hill dog. It was a white Burmese and had this bushy tail. She called it Snow. It only had three legs. She had rescued it on a mountain climbing trip with her father, near Darjeeling. She was very much like her father, you know. Augustus Holden - he was a gentle being. I think she inherited his kind-heartedness. That dog followed her everywhere with a look of worship in his eyes. I remember her telling me that her mother was furious when they brought it home to live with them. Lydia disliked dogs, and she threw an absolute fit and wouldn't hear of a dog staying in her house. So Celia tied Snow outside in the garden and just stopped eating. Lydia thought it was just a childish whim and let her be. Three days later, Celia fell terribly ill. Finally, the doctor told them that the child was not going to get any better if they couldn't get her to eat something. That was when Augustus put his foot down and, in the end, brought Snow into their house much against Lydia's wishes. There wasn't much Lydia could do about it. And Celia got what she wanted. Snow stayed with her."

"That's rather determined for a child. I've always felt that, for most children, the world is made up of bubbles of wants, and when one bubble bursts, it doesn't take a child long to forget it and follow another since there are so many floating around," Rachel said out loud.

"I'd say you were right, but it's no use trying to analyse Celia. She was no ordinary child. She always had the gift of focussing and getting whatever she wanted, even as a child. She'd always find a way others wouldn't dream of. Strange how fragile she looks, but I'd say there's a core of steel in that girl. Always has been."

"Most interesting," Jeremy said, looking intently at Dennis.

"I spent six consecutive summer vacations as a boy near Darjeeling at our tea estate, and Celia was always there. Looking back, I think I fell in love with her from the moment I set eyes on her. Even as a child, she was the most beautiful person I had ever met. She had the kind of natural beauty that simply took your breath away. And since we were the only two white children for miles we kept each other company most days. We would go walking up into the hills with her dog Snow in tow and have a small picnic with the boiled egg sandwiches and cake Lydia always packed for us. We talked about everything and laughed about everything. She was my golden girl. And when it would rain, we would sit watching the rain from the veranda in her house or mine. On sunny days, she loved to sit out in the garden and read. She would read out stories to me as we lay on the grass in the garden. We had the most marvellous time two children could have together, and just being with her or even knowing she was somewhere around, always made me feel complete.

Then in 1938, I was a freshman at Oxford and as usual went home for an Indian summer. It was the same year that Celia turned seventeen. Augustus Holden died in an unfortunate incident. There was a fire in the tea factory on their estate, and they found him charred to death along with a few other native workers who tried to douse out the flames. Somehow, her dog Snow must have followed her father into the factory and died in the fire along with him. Celia was inconsolable, and she just went into a shell. She didn't want to be with anyone, including me. She wouldn't even talk to me. It was like her world had ended. That was the worst summer of my life. Something changed between us. By fall, I had to go back to university, and I left India with a heavy heart. That's the last time I saw her in India.

The next summer I visited India, I heard that Lydia and Celia Holden had gone back to England and were living with some distant relatives up north. My mother informed me that Augustus Holden's death had left them very ill provided for, and both Lydia and Celia had to survive on the charity of their relations. It must have been quite a rotten time for them, especially through the war years. And after having lived such a good life on a tea estate where the tea company had provided them with every luxury and at least six servants. I tried getting her address and writing her, but all my letters always came back unopened. I tried asking every single one of my parent's friends, even old acquaintances at Darjeeling, if they knew where she was, but no one had any communication from them. I was desperately unhappy. I don't know how those years went by. Not a day went by that I didn't think of her.

Then a few years later, I was in London walking down Oxford Street one afternoon, and just as I turned onto Dering Street, I saw her coming out of MacCulloch and Wallis – the haberdashery store, with her mother. I was filled with joy. Quite overwhelmed. I couldn't believe my eyes. I ran up to them like a man possessed, as if they were a mirage and they would disappear if I took too long to reach them. Celia too seemed happy to see me. We exchanged pleasantries, and I asked them to come and have tea with me at the Corner House on Tottenham Court Road. Lydia said they had other things to do, but I pleaded desperately and she finally gave in.

I ordered our teas but the conversation was stilted since neither Celia nor I knew where to start. There was so much I wanted to say to her, and yet I found myself talking about silly things like the weather and types of tea! But after sometime, we got to talking about good times in Darjeeling and the ice was broken. Soon Celia and I were prattling on as if we were children again, back in India. Lydia sat quietly and just watched us talk. But I knew something was amiss. I finally asked her where they were staying, and she mentioned they were living here at Rutherford Hall and had come to London for a spot of trousseau shopping. *For Celia's upcoming wedding!* I felt as if I had been hit by a running train. I may have imagined it, but I looked at Celia and sensed a certain sadness in her eyes. Lydia told me that the engagement was announced in the Times, the week before last, and that Celia would be marrying Lord Charles Rutherford in a month's time. She promised to send me an invitation.

I was livid. I told Celia she would do no such thing! She was to marry me as soon as possible and that was it. I think I was shouting by then. Lydia asked me to keep my voice down. Everyone in that tea room had turned to stare at us. Lydia told me that if I truly loved Celia, I wouldn't stand in the way of her only chance at happiness. She reminded me that I was not in a position to ask for Celia's hand in marriage, that I was just a student with no income or inheritance and, pray, how did I think that I would be able to support or keep her daughter in comfort. I asked Celia if money was really that important to her and whether she was entering this marriage for her mother's sake. I could not believe that my sweet, unworldly and noble Celia would be willing to go into a loveless marriage just for the sake of money. It was beyond me, and I could not believe it. I beseeched her to marry me. I told her I'd get a decent job and try to make good by her if she'd only wait another year, for me to finish university.

Celia took my hand, and she looked at me point blank and said, 'Oh Dennis, my darling. I do so love you but it's no use. Please don't make a fuss. It's *awful* being poor and I hate it. *The only people who say money is not important are the ones who have it!* They don't know how awful it is to live without it. You have no idea what it's like for a girl to live in a horrible place with stinking shared bathrooms, in a dirty low class neighbourhood, never to have any luxuries or nice things, not to be able to go out and enjoy herself, to live day in and day out in dresses that a cousin or a friend handed down to you out of pity. It's a horrible and demeaning life. I am fed up with being poor, and I'm done with it. I want to live a good life. *I deserve to live a good life and so does Mummy*, and really Charles has been so kind to us. He's such a nice person. You would like him.' She had made up her mind. She was going to be Lady Charles Rutherford and that was it.

Lydia never sent me the wedding invitation. Nor did I mind. For I could not imagine anything worse than seeing my Celia being married off to some old fart of a Lord who was old enough to be her father. Sorry about that Rachel – I know he's your uncle and all that, but there it was. I took time off from university to spend a few months in Italy where I brooded about the injustice of it all for a while, and then I started writing. It was more like a catharsis to let go of my past and my heart-breaking loss. Celia had been my life. I had always thought we'd be together for the rest of our lives. And she was now married to someone else because he had more to offer her than I ever could. In losing Celia, I felt as if I'd lost an important part of myself, like a hand or a foot. I could never be the same again. Pain and inspiration just seemed to flow from my soul.

I wrote like a man possessed. I couldn't sleep. I couldn't eat. Nothing mattered except the words that flew out of my pen. It was as if a demon had taken over. I finished my book in three months. I had no mind to publish it. A year later, an old friend came to visit me in Florence and my manuscript was just lying about in the flat and he read it. He thought it was rather brilliant and asked me if he could send it to a publisher he knew. The book was accepted immediately by the publisher and to my surprise, went into print for several editions. And now, I never know what to say to reporters who come to do interviews with me without revealing a whole life's angst that led to me writing the book! Sometimes, I just want to shout out to them and say, 'Here I am, a sham. An author by default, who may never write another book again.' And the biggest joke of it all, is that I've been invited here to help Charles write his memoirs! Ha! The one man who took everything I had away from me. And the shame of it all is, that despite everything, I accepted his proposal just so I could see her once more and be near her again."

For the first time in her life, Rachel found herself at a loss for words. She didn't know what to say, so she just sat there, silently.

But Jeremy spoke up. "Nevertheless, if your passionate discourse is anything to go by, you do have a tremendous gift of expression, my boy. And you probably will write again, if that is your way to overcome a life crisis. Because in time, you'll find, that life is never smooth, and you never know what surprises it has in store for you, just around the corner," Jeremy said almost prophetically, as if he could see the events that were about to unfold.

Chapter Four

It was eight in the morning. Suzie, the parlourmaid, knocked on Rachel's bedroom door. She heard a sleepy voice say, "Come in," and entered with a tray of aromatic breakfast tea and toast. She walked to the window and placed the tray on the cushions near the bay windows, where she knew her mistress liked to sit, first thing every morning. Rachel loved to lounge on the cushions and look out into the flower garden below and the fields beyond while sipping her morning tea.

"Good morning Miss Rachel. It's such a sunny day today. Look Miss!" she said as she parted the pale rose silk drapes and fastened them to the ties on each side. Bright sunlight flooded the room in a haze of golden light.

"Good morning, Suzie. Looks like you brought sunshine in with you. How marvellous!" Rachel said, stretching luxuriously in her four poster bed before getting up to put on her robe.

Suzie giggled, "I thought you could use some sunshine Miss after all the terrible going ons yesterday."

"Indeed, we could all use some sunshine – today of all days dear Suzie. Any news from the kitchens?" Rachel asked.

"No Miss, but Mrs. Hopworth is all in a tizzy today and Betsy is so nervous that she already dropped Mr. Markham's breakfast tray and broke one of them china teapots. It's just that we've heard the *police are coming, Miss*. To the house to investigate! And we know what that means, Miss. They always hold the staff responsible for anything that goes wrong, they do!" Suzie said looking rather worried.

"Oh don't be silly Suzie. There's nothing to be nervous about. They'll probably just ask everyone in the house routine questions," Rachel said in a comforting voice.

"No, Miss. It happened to one of my friends Gracie who was in service down at Epsom Cottage in the village. Mrs. Thompson discovered that her diamond brooch was missing, and they called in the police to investigate. Gracie was booked for theft, Miss, seeing as she's the only one that works there. She swore she was honest as day and that she never took a thing. But they still hauled her off to the police station just the same and kept asking her if she wanted to confess. She kept crying and the sergeant told her it was no good crying and that she'd end up in jail for years and years if she didn't confess. So she did confess. But before she could come up for sentencing, Mrs. Thompson came by and said that it was all a mistake, and that she had found the brooch and it had got stuck by the pin to another dress in the wardrobe. They let Gracie go, but she's never been the same since," Suzie said with a sad face.

"Oh, but that's awful! And it's bullying! The police aren't supposed to do that. The poor girl. Being made to fess up to a theft she never committed. Don't worry, this is not the same thing. At any rate, I shan't let anyone bully you, Suzie, or the others. I promise you. Now come on, buck up and give us a smile."

"Right, Miss. Then I shan't worry." Suzie smiled wanly and started picking up clothing articles left in a heap on the floor and folded them neatly to tidy up the room.

II

Two doors down from Rachel's room, the other parlourmaid Betsy, knocked lightly on Lady Celia's door. There was no answer, but she could hear voices from within, and since no one else was about, she leaned forward to listen.

She heard Mrs. Lydia Holden's voice ring out in her usual sharp tone. "You are the most infernal child, Celia. It must've been a nightmare or just your overactive imagination. You always did live in a dream world, even as a girl. You imagine things. You always have!"

Then she heard Lady Celia's voice, sounding angry. "But I tell you *he was dead, Mother!* And there was so much blood on him and the rug. I even knelt down and touched him, and he was still warm. Ugh. It was awful!"

Then Lydia's voice rang out again. "You couldn't have possibly seen Charles dead in the study. There's no sign of his body, do you hear? And no sign of blood on any rug in the study, otherwise someone would've noticed.

Get a hold of yourself girl, before the police come and start asking questions. I'd advise you to keep mum about what you imagined you saw, because I tell you, it's not possible! It's probably those pills the doctor gave you last night. Most likely made you hallucinate. I've got to go and get ready before the police arrive. They'll be here any minute."

Betsy heard Lydia's footsteps approaching the door from within. She moved away so it would seem that she was just walking towards the door when Lydia came out of the room.

Lydia came out and gave Betsy a sharp look. "What are you doing here? Were you just listening at the door?" she asked accusingly.

"No, Ma'am, I would never do that!" Betsy said indignantly, defending her honour. "Just getting the Ladyship's morning tea, Ma'am."

"Alright, don't just stand there gawking at me, girl. Get on with your work," Lydia said sharply.

"Yes, Ma'am," she replied politely and, stepping forward, knocked loudly on Celia's door.

Chapter Five

At nine fifteen in the morning, Inspector Mathew Parker and Sergeant Steven Wilder were making their way towards Rutherford Hall in the police car. Inspector Parker was about 45, clean shaven and had a quiet way about him. He didn't look like a police officer at all. He was about 5' 8", slightly thick around the middle, had gentle brown eyes and a warm smile, and there wasn't much he didn't know about the people and events in the village. If he had been an actor, the director would've certainly cast him as the village baker or greengrocer without hesitation. The years in the force had made him an astute judge of human nature, and the fact that he didn't look the least bit threatening had always worked well in his favour. People tended to trust him, and his reputation in police circles was that, in the end, like the Canadian Mounties, *he always got his man.*

Sergeant Steven Wilder on the other hand, had a personality that was in complete contrast to his immediate superior. He was young, highly energetic and ambitious. He was six feet tall and quite well built. Cindy, the barmaid at the village pub who reportedly had a crush on him according to village gossip, had nicknamed him the 'Man Mountain', and the nickname had been so apt that it stuck. Without meaning to do so, he ended up intimidating a lot of people with his brash, no nonsense way of talking, and most suspects would break down easily within minutes when subjected to a questioning session by him. Even out of uniform, no one could mistake him for anything else other than a policeman. Inspector Parker was sure that Sergeant Wilder would go far in the police force, if he toned down his natural aggressiveness a notch. He had realised that underneath the brash exterior, there was a good deal of intelligence aided by an uncommon amount of common sense that resonated well with the Inspector's own cool, logical mind. Despite the differences in their personal style of going about police work, they made an excellent team and had a good deal of respect for each other's judgement when it came to solving cases, small or big.

They found Hopworth coming down the front steps as they drove up to the main entrance of the house.

"Good morning, Inspector," Hopworth said as he opened the car door on Inspector Parker's side.

"Morning, Hopworth. Lovely day today," said Inspector Parker acknowledging his greeting as he alighted from the car.

"It certainly is that, Sir." Hopworth replied with a smile and then looking at Sergeant Wilder still behind the wheel, said, "Hello, Steven. Good to see you again."

"Likewise, Mr. Hopworth. Hope Mrs. Hopworth is well, Sir," Sergeant Wilder enquired with a gentleness, that others were unaccustomed to hearing in his voice.

"Yes, Gladys is well. She's waiting to see you." Then, lowering his voice as Sergeant Wilder got out of the car and came to his side, Hopworth whispered, "She's been baking since seven in the morning. Made a batch of your favourite ginger biscuits for you," he told him conspiratorially.

Though Inspector Parker had walked up slightly ahead of them, he had heard Hopworth's last sentence and it made him smile. It was heart-warming and funny at the same time to witness the 'Man Mountain' turn into a shy little schoolboy in the presence of Hopworth.

Inspector Parker knew the whole story. Hopworth's son, Burt Hopworth, and Steven Wilder had been the best of friends since they were tots. They had not only been classmates and bench mates at school, but had been inseparable as they grew up. Both boys were high spirited and adventurous. They even looked like brothers, their features were so alike. Together, they had gotten into boyish scrapes and all kinds of mischief in the village after school hours. As they grew up into young adults, Steven had joined the police force and Burt had started work as a junior clerk in the local law firm - Graham, Bending & Grayson, thanks to a glowing character recommendation from Lord Rutherford. Five years ago, Burt Hopworth had been found guilty for fraud and embezzlement at the law firm and had been sentenced to three years of penal servitude. A common enough story - The son of honest, hardworking parents in domestic service, Burt was fed up of seeing his folks slave day in and day out their whole lives without having much to show for it in the end, except for respectability. Burt wanted to break out of this inherited mould of servitude and, unfortunately, chose the wrong way to get rich quick, with disastrous results for all concerned. It had been a terrible ordeal, not just for the Hopworths, but for Burt and Steven as well. Especially for Steven, as he had been on the other side of the law and was forced to stand and watch helplessly as his best friend was sent away to prison.

Burt had come out of prison two years ago, a changed, disillusioned and repentant man. He had come home to his parents at Rutherford Hall and tried to make amends. Hopworth had told him, in no uncertain terms and amidst much protest and crying on his wife Gladys' part, that he was no longer welcome to come home. Even Steven had tried to reconcile father and son, but Hopworth had said harshly, "He's a wrong 'un. There's something wrong about the way he thinks. There's a defect in his head. You both had the same upbringing, similar home life, education and a chance at a better life than we ever had. But that wasn't enough for him. How is it that you turned out well, Steven, and he became a thief, a petty criminal? I did the best I could for the boy. I will not blame myself or Gladys for how he turned out. He is no son of ours!" Steven had understood then that Hopworth had lived his entire life based on certain rigid values and principles that Burt had not only ridiculed, but also violated. Hopworth not only disowned his son, but forbade him to keep in touch with either him or his mother for the rest of their lives.

This sentence had seemed far worse to Burt and his mother Gladys than the sentence he had served by going to prison. Heartbroken, Burt had left the only place he had ever known as home and had gone into unfamiliar London to try and build his life from scratch. Jobs were difficult to come by, and he came to realize the harsh reality that, despite his educated upbringing, with a prison sentence under his belt, the only jobs that people would consider him for were the menial ones that no one else would be desperate enough to take up. Steven heard from him from time to time, as Burt kept moving from one menial job to another in London. Last heard, Burt had been employed as a dish washer in one of the seedier London hotels. His inheritance of servitude that he had tried so hard to break away from had now ironically become an undeniable part of his life.

Chapter Six

"The family is waiting for you in the sitting room, Inspector," Hopworth said as he led the way to the sitting room and announced them in.

"Ah, there you are, Inspector!" said James Markham as he walked up to shake his hand. "Allow me to introduce you to my wife Elizabeth. She's Lord Rutherford's sister, and, this is our daughter Rachel. And this is Mrs. Lydia Holden, Lady Celia Rutherford's mother. And Mr. Hawthorne."

"May I enquire where Lady Celia Rutherford is?" Inspector Parker asked James Markham.

Lydia spoke up, "My daughter had been advised bed rest by Doctor Devine, Inspector. She's recovering from yesterday's accident, which I'm sure you've heard about. It would be better if she's allowed to rest today," she said, sounding mildly authoritative.

"I've already had a word with the doctor, Mrs. Holden, regarding the accident last night. He believes Lady Celia may be able to throw a great deal of light on what happened yesterday. I'm afraid we will need to ask her a few questions," Inspector Parker said to her, quietly but firmly.

"Well then, if you must, you must," Lydia Holden replied looking rather uncomfortable.

Dennis intervened, "Will that be absolutely necessary Inspector? She is in no state to be badgered right now."

"Rest assured, there'll be no badgering *unless* we feel someone is deliberately trying to conceal something that may be pertinent to solving this case," he said in his usual quiet manner and then went on, "This is my colleague, - Sergeant Wilder." Inspector Parker introduced Sergeant Wilder to everyone in the room. He continued, "We are going to be working on this case together. If we are to find out where Lord Rutherford is, I expect everyone in the house to *fully cooperate* and share anything they know about last night's activities with Sergeant Wilder and myself," he said, looking around from face to face and then pointedly at Mrs. Holden and Dennis.

"Right, of course. Where would you like to start, Inspector?" James asked him.

"To begin with, we need a recent photograph so we can get the police sketches sent to our neighbouring police stations in the surrounding county. We'll also need a description of the clothes he was wearing when last seen."

"We can all probably give you a vague idea of how he was dressed when we saw him in the study, but he may have changed into evening attire or something else before leaving the house. I'll get Charles' valet to go through his wardrobe and see what's missing and what he may have worn last evening," Lydia said helpfully.

"That's good thinking Mrs. Holden. I appreciate it. We'll also need a list of all the people present in the house yesterday, including the list of dinner guests and a list of all household staff, and then we'll take it from there," Inspector Parker replied.

"I'll ask Hopworth to get the staff list together. We had hired some extra hands from the village last night to come up and help us with the party. I'm sure he will have all the details. As for the list of dinner guests...we did set the table for eighteen and I have place cards with everyone's names," Lydia Holden said.

Elizabeth Markham spoke up. "Rachel and I can help you get that list ready, Lydia. If there's anything else Inspector?"

Sergeant Wilder spoke up, his professional persona coming to the fore once more. "Yes, we'll need a room for the day where we can conduct interviews. Preferably semi-private. A place where we will not be disturbed or distracted while working on the case."

Dennis Hawthorne spoke up before anyone else could reply. "You could use the library, Sergeant, since the study table is completely choc-a-bloc full with my typewriter, writing material, mountains of family archives and albums of family history that I'm working on at the moment for Lord Rutherford's memoirs. The papers are in a certain order, and I would like to continue with my work today, if that's alright with you."

Sergeant Wilder replied, "The Library would suit us just fine. As long as you make yourself available for the interview, you can continue with your work Mr. Uh..."

"Hawthorne. Dennis Hawthorne." Dennis replied, thinking sardonically to himself...*so much for being a famous author*, and smiled inwardly.

"Good. That's settled then." James Markham spoke up.

"Right. We'll get on with the investigation then," said Inspector Parker.

Twenty minutes later the inspector and sergeant had organized the furniture in the library so they could start their questioning. Hopworth had provided them with a list of staff members, while Rachel had given them the rest of the list of family members and dinner guests that had been present in the house, the night before.

Sergeant Wilder was going through Rachel's list. He looked up from it and asked Inspector Parker, "The list mentions a Mr. Jeremy Richards. He's the only one on this list who seems to be new to these parts. What do we know about him, Sir?"

"Ah, yes Richards. You may not know this but he's one of us. Ex Scotland Yard. As shrewd and as tough as they come. A man of high intelligence and known to be completely fearless. He's been responsible for sending more blue blooded criminals to the gallows than the lot of them put together, up at the Yard. I can tell you for a fact that he rubbed quite a few people in high places the wrong way. He was responsible for finding that MP, Lord Heatherton, guilty in the Archer murder case. That must've been a tough one to crack."

"I remember the Archer case, Sir. Terrible. The nine-year-old schoolboy Percy Archer killed in cold blood because he had accidentally witnessed a murder committed by the MP," was Sergeant Wilder's response.

"Yes. They tried to pass it off as a kidnapping gone wrong, to save Heatherton's hide. Despite being given feelers from the powers that be, to go easy on the case, Detective Richards dug deeper and got to the bottom of it. He was the one that tracked the boy down to Heatherton's hunting lodge in the country. But he got there too late to save the child. The newspapers had reported that the boy's body was found in the woods about two miles from the hunting lodge. But they omitted mentioning the condition it had been found in. They were also forced to leave out the rest of the gory details, in view of the public furore it would have evoked and the subsequent damage it would have caused to the political party, Heatherton had an allegiance with, at the time. The details of the case were hushed up and the hush orders had come right from the top."

"Sir, if I may ask, how did you come to know so much about this case if it's not public knowledge?" Sergeant Wilder asked him with a puzzled look in his eyes.

"Let's just say that we have a circle of interested parties – some from the government and the judiciary and other involved sectors of law enforcement such as select members of the Scotland Yard, the police force and armed forces, which meet from time to time and discuss interesting business and political matters of the day. I am privileged to be a part of such a group."

"British Intelligence, you mean?" Sergeant Wilder looked at him in awe.

"Let's not jump to any conclusions here, Sergeant. Getting back to the Archer case and erstwhile Scotland Yard Detective Richards, the fact was the case was suppressed and pressure was brought in from a certain political party to hide the truth."

"What was the truth Sir?" Sergeant Wilder enquired.

"The truth that came out from the forensic investigation was that the little boy had been kept alive and brutally tortured for five long days before he was actually killed. Heatherton was a sadistic bastard. And he was smug enough to think that because of his position in high society and politics, no one would dare touch him. They say Richards never quite got over finding the nine-year-old boy's mutilated body. And then the coroner's report on what that small child had to endure before he was killed drove Richards completely over the edge. What you also may not know, because this bit never came out in the newspapers either, is that Richards deliberately went out of line from Scotland Yard procedure and as soon as he had solid evidence that Heatherton had been responsible for the boy's torture and death, he entered the man's house in Mayfair, ostensibly to arrest him, and systematically went to work beating him so that he would suffer maximum pain but not die. Richards was a thorough professional about it. Mind you, Lord Heatherton did not bleed externally or have a single visible cut on him, and yet his spine was broken in two places along with his arms and legs, and he was in a catatonic condition and in excruciating pain by the time the other officers arrived on the scene. He was paralysed waist down for the remainder of his existence and remained in considerable pain till they carried out the sentence and hung him for both the murders – the one that the boy had witnessed and the murder of the little boy. They say Richards took the heat for using excessive force with a claim of self-defence. The evidence coincided with his statement since Richard's left arm had been winged by a bullet from Heatherton's gun. But inside information says otherwise. That Richards did that to himself with Heatherton's gun just so he could mete out his own form of justice. You see, Richards had made no bones about his belief *that just hanging the man would have been too soft a punishment for what he had done to that child.* Soon after that, Richards took early retirement on medical grounds for the gunshot wound to his arm. Some say he was forced to retire, but I don't believe for a minute, that a man like that can be forced to do anything unless he wants to. The upshot is that Scotland Yard has lost one of their finest. But in a way, their loss is our gain, Sergeant, because the man in question is now a quiet and unobtrusive member of our little village here. He bought the 'Sunny Ridge' cottage eight months ago and is now a bonafide resident of this little community."

"And he just happened to be here last night when the only blue blood in a thirty mile radius went missing," Sergeant Wilder said softly, as if he were thinking out loud.

"No, I don't believe he had anything to do with that. I may have done him an injustice by making him sound like a dangerous lunatic in my discourse, but Richards is far from that. He has a very strong sense of fair play and justice, and he's not the sort of person who would target anyone just because of their lineage," Inspector Parker responded.

"What if, Lord Rutherford had skeletons tumbling out of his closet? Most old families do have a skeleton or two, you know, and what if Richards had found something disturbing and decided to dispense his own style of justice once again?" Sergeant Wilder asked.

"You could be right. We can't discard any theory at the moment but it won't do, to go off on a wild goose chase when there are logical methods available at hand, to get to the bottom of this," Inspector Parker replied.

Chapter Seven

James Markham was seated in the library and giving his rendition of the events that took place the night before.

He sounded a trifle vague. "I remember taking a walk before six. Then I came into the study through the French windows..."

"The French windows were open? In the dismal weather there was last night?" Sergeant Wilder cut in, looking puzzled.

"No, they were fastened shut, but they were never locked until bedtime so that people can stroll about and go out or come in as they please. Lord Rutherford saw to that. He even had a coat rack with a few old coats placed in the study so one could just nip out without having to bother with getting their coats from the cloakroom near the hall. He was a great one to just nip out for a short walk around the grounds whenever he felt like it, and the staff had been instructed to leave the French windows to the study and the library unlocked at all times of the day except for when everyone turned in for the night," James replied.

"Interesting. I'll make a note of that. So you came in through the French windows and then?" Sergeant Wilder said, prompting James Markham to continue with his version of events.

"Well. Let's see...I came in and saw Charles hard at work, dictating his memoirs and Dennis sitting and banging away at the typewriter taking notes for the book, presumably. I said something to the effect that they had better get a move on if they wanted to be ready for the dinner party on time. And Charles replied that he wanted to finish 1925 before they would call it a day. Since they were engrossed in work, I went up to take a bath and then came down to see if I could help with something."

"What time would that be, Major Markham?" Inspector Parker asked.

"About 6:45 I reckon. The study door was ajar, and I could hear the boy still banging away at the typewriter and Charles' voice droning on, so I went into the sitting room but no one was there. I checked in the formal dining room and that seemed to be a beehive of activity, with Lydia shouting out instructions and those maids running about with bits of cutlery and placing wine glasses and all that sort of thing. Didn't want to get in their way so I went back out into the hall and met Celia coming down the stairs. She looked absolutely stunning. I told her as much. That girl is a sight for sore eyes, I can tell you Inspector," James said with a dreamy smile on his face.

Sergeant Wilder cut in a trifle briskly, "How your sister-in-law looks is not a matter of investigation here, Mr. Markham."

"No. No of course. I get your point. Quite," James said, slightly flustered.

"Can you tell us if she was behaving normally, not excited or depressed about anything?" asked Inspector Parker.

"Come to think of it, yes, she did look slightly worried about something. In fact I asked her if everything was alright and she said sort of hesitatingly, 'It's nothing. Just the usual domestic things,' or something to that effect. And then she looked worried again and asked me, 'James, have you seen my mother anywhere?' And I replied that I had seen Lydia in the formal dining room organizing everything, busy with last minute dinner settings. 'Oh! She's alright then,' she said, as if she seemed relieved about something. Then, as an afterthought, she enquired about Charles, and I told her that he and Dennis were still busy with the writing work and she didn't seem to mind. By then both Elizabeth and Rachel came downstairs, dressed for dinner and she told them, 'You and Rachel must help me greet the guests. They'll be here any minute. Mother is tied up and Charles and Dennis have absolutely no sense of time!'"

"What time were the guests expected?" Sergeant Wilder asked.

"7:30 pm. But you know how it is over here, Inspector, most people in the village like to be punctual and arrive a few minutes before time. Let me see...yes. At about 7.15 onwards, the guests started arriving. The Vicar and his wife Margery arrived along with the Weatherbys - John and Linda. Then five minutes later, the Thompsons arrived with the Doctor's wife Mary Devine. The Doctor was on a case five miles away and would be joining us later, so Mary had taken a lift with the Thompsons. Elena and Robert Wickham were the last to arrive. Hopworth and Suzie came in with a round of drinks and some hors d'oeuvres, and we all helped ourselves. We all sat about and chatted. I remember I was quite amused by how anxious the middle aged Georgina Thompson was, to meet Dennis Hawthorne – *the famous novelist*, as she put it. I had no clue that boy's book was so popular! She said she had been looking forward to meeting him for days. Funny, how these fat little women always behave like idiotic schoolgirls around writers and the artistic types. She went on and on about how excited she was about finally being able to meet a famous author in flesh and blood, and about how marvellous his book was and how tragic it was, and how she had wept like a child when the hero died in the end and all that sort of nonsense. Then Lydia joined us and I overheard Celia asking her whether she had seen Charles, and Lydia answered that she had seen him and Dennis about fifteen minutes ago in the study before she had gone upstairs to freshen up for the party. Celia looked worried and excused herself, to go and check on Charles and Dennis and see what was taking them so long. Right after that, about ten minutes later, Dennis joined us and was positively bulldozed by that Thompson woman as soon as he came in."

"What time was that?" Sergeant Wilder asked. He was taking down notes.

"Ah, yes, I remember telling the old girl, my wife that is, that it wasn't like Charles to be so late for his own party. The hall clock had sounded its half hourly chime just some time before, so must have been 7:45 or, at the most 7:50 pm."

"When did the accident take place?" Inspector Parker asked him.

"Round about the same time. It's quite extraordinary. Celia had gone to check on Charles. The first place she was likely to look in was the study. But instead, she somehow managed to get onto the driveway and under Jeremy Richard's car!"

"What do you think could have happened?" Inspector Parker asked.

"I really can't be sure, but my best guess would be that she found Charles wandering about outside the French windows or probably saw him walking out somewhere, and she followed him outside to remind him about the party but got hit by the car before she could catch up with him. The only logical explanation I can think of."

"That doesn't sound right somehow. Surely, if Lord Rutherford was walking on the driveway presumably towards the gate to go somewhere, he would have had to cross Jeremy Richards driving up in his car, and Mr. Richards would have mentioned something about it since you all were so anxious to find him," was Inspector Parker's response to James Markham's half-baked theory.

"I suppose so," James said, looking flustered again.

"Besides, it doesn't explain the blood on her hands," Sergeant Wilder added.

"No, I suppose not. I can't think how that happened," James Markham said to the officers.

"What happened next?" Inspector Parker asked.

"Hopworth came into the formal sitting room where the party was going on and came up to me and told me in a hushed sort of voice that Lady Celia had been in an accident and if I would like to come and help. Dennis was standing close by, being mauled by that Thompson creature, and overheard what Hopworth said to me. I took the old girl, my wife, aside and told her what had happened and asked her to hold the fort while Dennis and I excused ourselves and followed Hopworth into the hall, where we saw Richards standing with Celia in his arms. He looked terribly apologetic, and he explained what had happened... how she simply ran in front of his car and that there was nothing he could have done about it and all that. She was unconscious, and had blood on her. We – that is, Dennis and I, decided to carry her upstairs to her bedroom, and then Lydia or someone or other rang for the doctor. You know the rest," James Markham said.

"Yes, well. Thank you Major Markham. Could you request Lady Elizabeth to come and see us?" Inspector Parker said, adding "And please don't go anywhere today. We may need to ask you more questions later."

"Right-O! I'll be around and about if you need me, Inspector," James Markham replied.

Chapter Eight

Elizabeth Markham walked into the library and asked, "You wanted to see me, Inspector?" She was dressed simply in a sensible grey tweed skirt suit with a white silk blouse and a string of pearls. Even in that simple attire, she managed to look as elegant and graceful as she had looked in her formal evening gown the night before.

"Yes, I did. Please make yourself comfortable, Lady Elizabeth," Inspector Parker said politely, showing her to an armchair. He found himself thinking, *There is something about the way she walks and holds herself upright, that one can tell at a glance, here is a woman who is descended from a long line of aristocratic ancestors.*

She sat down and said, "Thank you." And then added matter-of-factly, "I'm sure you will want to hear about the sequence of activities I participated in, last evening."

"Yes, we would be most obliged if you could tell us how last night's events unfolded, in your own words," Inspector Parker said as he sat down in an armchair opposite her.

Sergeant Wilder was standing, resting his back to the wall, quietly observing them.

"Good. I thought as much. To save us both some time, I've written everything down in as much detail as I could remember along with the timelines in which all the events took place," she said, handing over a folded piece of notepaper to the inspector that she had taken out from her jacket pocket.

"That is most helpful Lady Elizabeth and indeed quite thoughtful," Inspector Parker said, as he took the notepaper and glanced at it. Everything was neatly listed in a clear flowing handwriting. Each sentence began with a time jotted down followed by what took place. *A cool, calculating mind most women would envy. Quite a contrast to that blundering husband of hers.*

"Well, I shall get on with my work then, Inspector. I have, rather a lot to do today. Unless there is something else you would like to know?" she asked, as she got up to leave.

"Lady Elizabeth, there are a few other things which I was hoping you could help me with, if you don't mind..." he said gently in a charming voice, motioning her to sit down.

"Not at all. What is it you wish to know?" she asked him as she fell back in her armchair.

"A few things have been puzzling me. They are slightly personal, so I sincerely hope that you do not take offence."

"That depends on what you would like to know," she said giving a half smile.

"For one, I would like to enquire how long you have been staying at Rutherford Hall," he asked.

"That's easy - for about a year," she replied.

"It would also interest me to learn why you and your family have been living here at your brother's home for the past year," he asked.

"Now that is a rather personal question, and I would tell you only if you can tell me what bearing it has on the current investigation, Inspector," she asked, with a touch of irritation in her voice.

"My dear lady. The last thing I want to do is to offend you in any way. The reason I asked is because I think it may have some bearing on this case and Lord Rutherford's state of mind at the time of his disappearance. But if you choose not to answer the question or feel that it is an inappropriate one, please accept my sincere apologies," Inspector Parker said in his usual quiet voice.

"Then, at the risk of sounding rude, I choose not to answer it, Inspector," she said, as she got up haughtily. And then a change came over her face, and she sat back in the arm chair heavily. "Oh, what's the use! With a little superficial digging, you'll probably find out anyway. It's common enough knowledge in London."

"Is it a change in circumstances, perhaps?" Inspector Parker asked intuitively, with a quiet concern in his voice.

"Yes, if you can call it that. My father settled a great deal of money on me when I married James. He was a dashing young army officer and I was a foolish young girl. My father was not a Victorian man. He believed that daughters had the same amount of intelligence and decision making capabilities as sons. He asked me if I was absolutely sure that James was the man I wished to spend the rest of my life with, and when I said yes, he simply gave us his blessings and handed over my inheritance to us so we could embark on our married life. Being young and foolish, a dangerous combination if I may say so, I allowed my gallant husband to take control of all our money and investments. It may be hard to believe, but James managed to invest our money, bit by bit, in every unwise investment opportunity that came up. We suffered one debilitating loss after another. Until there was nothing left. A year ago, we not only lost everything we had but also found ourselves knee deep in debt. We had to sell everything, almost all of my mother's jewellery, our house in Kensington Gardens, even the car," Elizabeth said, looking down at her hands on her knees.

"I have nothing but the greatest respect for you, Lady Elizabeth, to be able to counteract such a blow with such cool and calm acceptance," Inspector Parker said, with a great deal of admiration in his voice.

"There is not much else anyone can do given the circumstances, Inspector," she said with a wan smile, and added, "If you find me calm in the face of financial adversity, Inspector, it is only because it is much easier to withstand a misfortune such as this when my family and I are still ensconced in the lap of luxury, thanks to a generous and understanding brother like Charles. It would be unfair on my part to take any credit; after all, adversity is the easiest thing to bear when every luxury in life is granted you."

"Thank you, Lady Elizabeth, for being so forthright. I will not keep you any longer from your daily duties," Inspector James replied.

"Please find Charles, Inspector," she said getting up from the armchair, holding his gaze. And then she stopped at the study door and looked back at him, "At any rate, *please find out what happened to him.* For all our sakes," she said, before leaving the room.

Inspector Parker found himself thinking that Lady Elizabeth Markham was indeed a remarkable woman.

Chapter Nine

Sergeant Wilder was on a mid-morning tea break and was sitting at the kitchen table with a plate of ginger biscuits and a cup of tea in front of him. He had come down to meet Gladys Hopworth, his best friend Burt's mother and the cook at Rutherford Hall. He was very fond of Gladys and had enjoyed being at the receiving end of her superlative baking skills ever since he had been a schoolboy in shorts. She had been looking forward to his visit and had welcomed him with a warm embrace.

"And how is your dear mother, Steven?" Gladys enquired with a smile.

"Oh, she's very well, Mrs. Hopworth. Both my Mum and Dad are still on a holiday in Blackpool. I thought my mother could use a break. So I booked them into that fancy new resort hotel that's come up, by the sea. She made a fuss about it initially. You know how she is, about my spending money on them. But I saw them off on the train to Blackpool ten days ago and they're having a jolly time," he said, crumbling a biscuit between his fingers and eating the crumbs out of habit.

"How lovely! You are a good boy, Steven. Let me get you some more tea, and we'll have a good old chat like in the old days," she said, as the kettle came to a boil and started whistling.

"Been looking forward to it. It's been ages since I caught up with you," Sergeant Wilder said.

"So...how did you suddenly come up with the idea of sending them to Blackpool?" she asked him, re-filling his cup with fresh tea.

"Well. This winter's been so cold and my Mum was suffering more than usual from her rheumatism. It's got worse over the years, you know. And I got absolutely fed up of seeing her work so hard. The woman doesn't know the meaning of the word rest!" he told her.

"It's very thoughtful of you, to give them a treat like that. Doris must love it there," she said with a smile.

"Got a postcard from her just yesterday. She says she's having the time of her life. She wrote that she and Dad were bullied into dancing the tango one evening by the dance hostess at their hotel! I can just picture them at it!" he said smiling widely.

"It does my heart good to hear about it," she said smiling back.

Lowering his voice, he asked, "Have you had any news from Burt lately?"

"It's best we don't bring up his name. His father will have my hide if he finds me talking about him, even with you!" she said in a hushed voice, trying to evade any further talk about Burt.

At that moment, the parlourmaid, Betsy, came in and saw Sergeant Wilder and said to him, "Thank God, it's you Steven and not that other bully of a sergeant, *what's-his-name Harolds*, who booked our Gracie for theft!"

"I think Sergeant Harolds was just doing his job like the rest of us. Anyhow, Inspector Parker asked for me specifically to help him on this case *seeing that I have connections here.* And I'm glad he did. Wouldn't have missed these ginger biscuits for the world!" he said, smiling at Gladys.

"Always nice to see the *Man Mountain* tucking in. Need to be ship-shape for all the dances he's been attendin'. I met Cindy a couple of months ago, and she was in a right tizzy over some dance you were taking her out to," Betsy said saucily.

"Steven! You never told me that you and Cindy were steppin' out together!" Gladys said teasingly, and continued, "You used to tell me things as a boy, and now that you're all grown up, you forget to tell me that you have a girlfriend?!" she added in a mock hurt tone.

"It was just one blooming dance! She dumped me after that anyhow, for some other fellow..." he replied turning beetroot red and grumbled, "Don't understand why women make such a bloomin' song and dance about every little thing a man does!"

Betsy replied in a placating tone, "Now, now. We were just teasin' you, so stop getting all worked up.

And what were you doing here last night? I thought I saw you in the back garden just before the guests started coming in."

"Me? You saw me here last night? No. You must've mistaken someone else for me," Sergeant Wilder said, looking nonplussed.

"Looked like you from the back anyhow. Ah well! Could have been someone else, I suppose. In all that fog and coming and going, must've made a mistake. Never mind," Betsy said.

"Don't know anyone else around here who looks half as good as me though!" Sergeant Wilder replied tongue-in-cheek.

"Ah well. It's me eyes. Probably need glasses. I remember always getting mixed up with you and Burt, when you boys used to hang about here." Then addressing Gladys, she added in a falsetto, "Oh, and Mrs. Hopworth, Queen Mary wants to see you in her chambers now. She said she *wanted to consult you over the menu for tonight's dinner*," she said, mocking an upper class accent.

"Well, she can bloody well wait. Tell her I'm busy talking to the sergeant here," Gladys replied in an irritable tone.

"Right! I will inform her highness that you are currently occupied with important police business and cannot be disturbed." Then giggling at her own wit, Betsy did a mock curtsey and left the kitchen.

"Queen Mary?" asked Sergeant Wilder with one raised eyebrow.

"That's Mrs. Lydia Holden, the Ladyship's mother. Queen Mary is what the entire staff calls her. She's the most insufferable woman. Always poking about and trying to boss over everyone. It's a shame how she lords it around in her daughter's marriage, and she has no business even staying in this house! Got nowhere to go. Poor as a church mouse, and she has the nerve to swan about as if she owns this place! I tell you, she has no business to even live here, let alone try and get all bossy with the lot of us."

"What's she done to get all your backs up?" Sergeant Wilder asked her.

"It's just her high handedness, and the way she treats people like dirt. The staff can't stand her anyhow. She is also the most petty-minded woman I have ever come across. She's probably never seen this kind of money being spent on a kitchen or on the staff, and calls it daylight robbery! Keeps checking kitchen accounts and, would you believe it, yesterday, she even tried to get me to shift to cheaper second grade ingredients for the party to save money. But I told her off right proper, I did! The nerve she has!"

"What did you tell her?" Sergeant Wilder asked, amused at the picture that was forming in his mind, of an indignant Gladys being told to use low grade ingredients in her cooking.

"I told her that, as long as I was Cook at the Rutherford household, Sir Charles and his guests would only be served meals that contained the finest ingredients that money can buy. And that she could consult Sir Charles if she thought otherwise," Gladys said in a huff.

"Put the woman in her place, huh?" he said smiling at her.

"Well. She said she would have a word with her daughter and make sure that my nose would be out of the joint if I kept spending this much money in the kitchen. And I told her she could go to the blazes and that I would be giving in my notice to Lady Celia if I was going to be harassed all the time by her mother!"

"What happened after that?" Sergeant Wilder asked.

"I dropped everything I was doing in preparation for the party and trotted right up to Lady Celia's room and spoke to her. Thank God she's nothing like her mother!"

"What's she like?" he asked her.

"Oh! Lady Celia is something else. A real lady, if you know what I mean. And such a sweet young lady. Really! How she turned out to be so nice with a mother like that has always been a wonder to me. After that row I had with her mother, I was ready to hand in my notice and went to speak to her about it, and she was ever so nice. She said to me, 'But Mrs. Hopworth, you've been here forever. This house will never run without you, don't you see? You can't leave. You are such a comfort to me, and to all of us. It's such a relief for me that I can leave the running of the kitchen in your capable hands. I wouldn't know the first thing about managing servants if you and Mr. Hopworth weren't there. I'm sure we'll be completely lost if you leave. So you see, you can't give notice! Especially not on account of my mother. I know she can be trying at times, but do try and be kind to her Gladys, for my sake, if nothing else. You see, my mother has had ever such an awful time since my father died. Look, I promise to have a word with her if you promise to stay! You will stay, won't you

Mrs. Hopworth. Please say you will,'" Gladys said, concluding her narration.

"Good for you! She sounds like a sensible woman to me. And she's right. Can't think of anyone who would do a better job of running this place other than you and Mr. Hopworth," Sergeant Wilder said, forming a favourable opinion about Celia Rutherford in his mind.

Chapter Ten

It was twelve noon. Jeremy Richards was driving back to Rutherford Hall to meet Inspector Parker. He had gotten a call from Inspector Parker earlier in the day requesting a meeting, and they had decided to meet at Rutherford Hall. Late last night, he had driven back from the hall to his cottage. Sleep had eluded him and, at about 2 am, he found himself wide awake again. When he finally managed to get some sleep, strange and vaguely erotic dreams featuring a faceless, nameless woman disturbed his peace of mind. In the dream, as he made love to this woman, a dark mist rose from nowhere, surrounded them, and slowly, as if she herself was made from vapour, the woman disappeared. He could not see anything, but could hear unfamiliar female voices in distress calling out repeatedly for help. After his restless night, he woke late, bathed and dressed and started back to meet the inspector. Jeremy was feeling slightly tired as he drove back to the hall and that surprised him, since his body had been used to keeping very odd timings. Lack of sleep had never been an issue for him. Back in Scotland Yard, he had been nicknamed *the bullterrier* because once he was on the scent of a kill, nothing else mattered. Even otherwise, eating and sleeping had always been low on his priority list. He had a reputation of working 36 to 48 hours at a stretch on a case and still have energy left over. *Must be getting soft in my old age*, he thought, smiling to himself. Rachel had also rung to inform him that she was having a place set for him at lunch since the inspector had informed her of his visit to the hall. He had accepted with gratitude.

He was greeted by Rachel as soon as he parked the car outside the entrance. She looked very different from the night before. She was dressed in a smart, apricot cashmere skirt jacket, which made her contrasting sea green eyes stand out. Jeremy noticed that she had no makeup on today, and she looked lovely, *like the proverbial English rosebud*. Her natural vitality and enthusiasm for life gave her a naturally pleasing vibrancy and a youthful glow. She was all peaches and cream under the mid-morning sun.

"Hello, I saw you drive up. I do like your car!" she said, as she came down the steps.

"Bought it a few months ago. Found it impossible to get about in the country without a car," he said.

"Yes, it's rather a pain. Always nice to own a set of wheels, especially one like this. Would simply love to have one of my own someday."

"Why don't you ask your father for a car this Christmas?" Jeremy asked with a smile.

"I would, if he had any money. We're stony broke, you know. Oh, we used to have pots and pots but my dear old Sadim went and lost it all," Rachel said, making a face.

"And Sadim would be...?" Jeremy asked, puzzled.

"My dear old Daddy of course. I call him Sadim because it's Midas spelt backwards. And he does rather have the Sadim touch. Everything he touches seems to turn to dust!" she said, laughing facetiously about it.

"Sorry. I didn't know about that," Jeremy said, sounding apologetic.

"How could you? One look at Mums and most people get the impression that we're loaded. And to be honest, they aren't very off the mark. My mum's side of the family is still pretty loaded, and if anything should've happened to Uncle Charles, we should be alright again...Uh oh. That came out sounding awful. Sorry! Didn't mean for it to come out like that but...!" Rachel faltered.

Jeremy rescued her by saying, "I know what you mean. Sometimes the truth, when put bluntly, can sound quite terrible. Tell me, has anyone ever advised you to cultivate a little diplomacy?" he asked her with a smile he could not repress.

"That's just it...I've always been awful at putting things across. Far too idiotic to be diplomatic. Uncle Charles used to joke about it, and say that the foreign office could use a few people like me!" she replied with a grimace.

"Yes, if they wanted one International crisis after another, I'd reckon you would be perfect for the job!" Jeremy said, chuckling.

Hopworth greeted Jeremy as they walked into the hall. "Good morning, Mr. Richards."

"Good morning, Hopworth. I hope Lady Celia is better today?"Jeremy enquired.

"Yes Sir. I am told that the Ladyship will be joining the family for lunch today. And Inspector Parker requested that I show you to the library as soon as you came in," Hopworth said.

"Right! He certainly doesn't want to waste any time," Jeremy said, looking at Rachel.

"Oh, I'll show Mr. Richards to the library," Rachel said to Hopworth, as she took Jeremy's arm.

"Very good, Miss," Hopworth replied as he retreated.

As they walked into the library together, Rachel made introductions. "Hello Inspector, I've caught the suspect you wanted for questioning. Found him loitering about suspiciously around the driveway. Says his name is Jeremy Richards."

"Guilty as charged! Good morning Inspector. It's nice to finally meet you," Jeremy said, smiling and holding his hand out.

"A pleasure, Detective Richards, your reputation at the Yard precedes you. This is my colleague Sergeant Wilder," Inspector Parker said, shaking his hand and introducing Jeremy to Sergeant Wilder.

"Good to meet you Detective Richards. Inspector Parker here has the highest regard for you," Sergeant Wilder said, holding his hand out.

"Delighted Sergeant! By the way, as you both must be aware, I am no longer a detective. Please feel free to call me Richards," he said, as he shook Sergeant Wilder's hand. Then, turning to Inspector Parker, he said with a smile, "You seem to have quite the team here."

"Now, if we could only enlist a brain like yours, I'm sure we'll get to the bottom of this business here in no time, Mr. Richards," the Inspector said, acquiescing to Jeremy's request.

"You flatter me, Inspector. I haven't been near a case for over a year now. I'm afraid my brain has gone quite soft with the good country life here. That said, it's all yours to pick in any which way you like," Jeremy said.

After the introductions were over, Rachel excused herself from the library. She had told Jeremy earlier on their way to the library that she had important business to attend to - "I shall be spending the day with my nose buried in a new mystery novel I just got my hands on. It's rather exciting and perfectly gruesome. Perhaps I'll find some good detecting tips in it that will help solve our own home grown mystery!"

"Yes, that ought to keep you out of trouble for a while!" he had said to her, with a smile on his face. He was beginning to like her, and to his own surprise, found that her company infused him with a contagious *'joie de vivre'* that had been missing from the boredom and practicality of his life post retirement.

Sergeant Wilder had just finished updating the inspector and Jeremy on what he had heard from the cook, Gladys Hopworth, regarding Mrs. Lydia Holden, when Suzie, the parlourmaid, knocked and came into the library.

"Sir, I wonder if I could have a word with you. You see, Betsy, the other parlourmaid, told me that

Mrs. Hopworth and Sergeant Wilder talked about Mrs. Holden, and I wondered if what I overheard yesterday may help you. Not that it has anything to do with Lord Rutherford disappearing like that last night, to my mind."

"Well, any information, however irrelevant, may be helpful to us at this point. Go on girl, what is it you overheard?" Inspector Parker asked.

"I don't know for sure if it has anything to do with all that's been going on, but I heard Lady Celia giving it good to that Mrs. Holden about messin' with the staff, Sir," she said.

"You mean they had a row?" Jeremy asked.

"Well, it was a big blow up if you know what I mean. Now, I'm not one to listen in to someone's private conversation *like some others I know.* It ain't ladylike and all that, but I couldn't help over hearing, seeing as, Mrs. Holden was screeching just like a banshee," Suzie replied, her eyes saucer like.

"Ahem." Inspector Parker cleared his throat, trying to keep a straight face. "Where were you when you heard this...ahem...screeching?"

"In the parlour, Sir. You see, Mrs. Holden's room is on the first floor where all the family bedrooms are, and hers is right above the parlour. The windows must have been open, Sir," she replied.

"Right. And what time did this big blow up, as you put it, take place?" the Inspector asked her.

"Well, Sir, it was at about four thirtyish in the afternoon, and I was just getting the tea things ready and all, when I heard Lady Celia's voice say,

'Mother please stop antagonizing the servants. Gladys wanted to leave!'

And Mrs. Holden said something like, 'How dare she speak to you about that. Anyway, it'll be a good thing if that wretched woman does leave. She doesn't know her place or how to take orders.'

Then Lady Celia told her something like, 'It's not your place to order people around Mother!'

And she said, 'How dare you speak to me like that? I have every right to speak my mind in my daughter's house!'

And Lady Celia told her angrily, 'Its Charles' house! And you have no business trying to run it.'

And then that Mrs. Holden screeched, 'If you were a better housekeeper, I wouldn't have to! Left to you, the servants would rob us blind!'

Then I heard the Ladyship raise her voice and tell her off big time, 'Let me remind you, Mother, it's not your house, and it's not your money. Do you understand? As it is, Charles is probably irritated with you. He was just telling me the other day that he's been getting nothing but complaints ever since you began interfering with running this house and the way you've been treating the staff. They've been here for years, Mother. If you continue this way, you will upset Charles a great deal and I won't have it!'

Then I heard that Mrs. Holden say, 'So that's it. You and Charles don't want me here!'

And then Lady Celia said all ladylike again, 'I didn't say that mother, but please stop running the house and the servants as if you own the place. Why can't you just spend your time relaxing, reading or meeting friends?'

Then Mrs. Holden said in a saucy voice, 'You mean, be as idle as you?'

And then the Ladyship really gave it to her, 'That's enough, Mother! You've always been judgmental about me. I will not stand for it any longer. I agree I'm not a good housekeeper. I never claimed to be! And as for being idle, if you think me idle, so be it! I will be as idle as I want to. It's my life and at least I don't go about behaving in a ridiculous way with the servants. Don't you see? They laugh behind your back!'

Then I heard Mrs. Holden sniffling like and she said, 'Oh! What a cruel thing to say, you ungrateful child! After all that I have done for you!'

And then the Ladyship said rather tartly, 'What exactly have you done for me, mother?'

Mrs. Holden shouted at her, *'If it weren't for me, you wouldn't be here! I made it all happen so that you could be comfortable!* Anyway, I will not stay where I'm not wanted and will leave as soon as I can.'

Then Lady Celia shouted back at her, 'Feel free to mother! If you really want to go back living in those two penny quarters you could afford for the past seven years, you are welcome to. I've done my best to help you, and there's only so much one can do to help those who won't help themselves. I'm done with helping you!'

That was it Sir and I think Lady Celia had left Mrs. Holden's room because I could hear her sniffling some more, but there was no more talk."

"Thank you er..." the inspector faltered.

"Suzie, Sir," she said, helping him out.

"Well, Suzie. You were right in coming to us. I don't know that this has any bearing on the case in hand at the moment, but you never know. It's a good thing you shared this with us. At least we know that you can be our eyes and ears around the house. And that is always helpful," the inspector told her kindly.

"Right, Sir! You can depend on me for that," Suzie said, all puffed up with the pride of having done her duty, and left the room.

"So what do you make of it?" Inspector Parker asked Jeremy and the Sergeant after Suzie had left.

"Well, it could be important," Jeremy said and added, "Perhaps, Lady Celia said something about it to Lord Rutherford. But no... It's too trivial a domestic issue to have bothered him. Any man in his right mind would've just shrugged it off as just one of those womanly episodes."

"But the good news is that it does coincide with Markham's story about Lady Celia being worried about her mother when she came downstairs before the party started. So Markham isn't quite off the bat as we thought him to be," Inspector Parker said, looking at Sergeant Wilder.

"Yes. It fits in with his story alright," was Sergeant Wilder's response.

"I think it's time we had a word with Mrs. Lydia Holden. We've been hearing rather a lot about the woman lately. In all fairness, it's time that we heard her side of things before we come to any conclusions about her and whether she had any role to play in Lord Rutherford's disappearance," Inspector Parker said.

"If I had a mother-in-law like that I'd have done a disappearing act long ago!" Sergeant Wilder said, his eyes twinkling in a rare display of humour.

Chapter Eleven

Lydia Holden walked in to the library. Her posture was erect and she was dressed in a badly cut cheap attire of a longish brown wool skirt and a blue printed blouse with a dark brown cardigan thrown over it. Her mousy hair was tied untidily and she wore no jewellery. The inspector looked at her and thought, *The first woman I've seen in this house who has positively no sense of style whatsoever.*

"Yes, Inspector, what can I do for you? Hopworth told me that you asked for me," she said, as she walked in and sat down.

"Well, yes, we did, Mrs. Holden. I assume you've met Mr. Richards?" the inspector asked.

"Of course I have. Met him last night. He was the one that ran over my daughter!" she replied.

"I assure you that it was purely by accident, a concatenation of circumstances with no malicious intent on my part, Mrs. Holden," Jeremy set about reassuring her.

"It never is, Mr. Richards. That's why one calls it an *accident*. Unless of course, *you are a psychopath and purposefully wanted to kill my daughter*," she said, looking at him with her head tilted to one side.

"Now, what made you think of that, Mrs. Holden?" Inspector asked her, curious to know what was going on inside her mind.

"One does read about such things these days. Anyway, that's neither here nor there. So what is it you want, Inspector? I do have work to do you know," she said, looking at him directly.

"Ah yes. We were given to believe that you had quite a row with your daughter yesterday and wanted to know if there was any basis to what we heard," the inspector asked her, getting to the point.

"How would you know about that? You'd think the walls were made out of paper in this house!" she said, frowning.

"It seems that your windows were open at the time, and one of the staff overheard," he said plainly.

"Must be that busybody good-for-nothing cook. She's got her knife into me for some reason. Resents anything I say. Servants these days!" she said, ranting out her frustration.

"As a matter of fact, it was not Mrs. Hopworth who repeated the incident to us but one of the parlourmaids," Inspector Parker said, correcting her assumption.

"Must be that Betsy then. Always eavesdropping on everyone. I caught her listening outside Celia's room this very morning," Lydia said.

"Well, never mind who it was. Is it true?" asked the inspector, in a slightly irritable tone.

"I would think, Inspector, that you had far more important things to think about than giving importance to a mother-daughter disagreement over a simple domestic issue! For instance, has Dennis told you about that note I found in the pantry yesterday?" Lydia Holden said tartly, turning the tables on him.

"No, I haven't had a chance to have a word with Mr. Hawthorne yet. What note would that be?" the inspector queried.

"It was a crumpled up piece of rough paper that said, *'Meet me behind the summer house at seven pm. Bring the money with you. Burt.'* Rather sinister, don't you think? Must've fallen out of that cook's apron pocket," she said.

"What makes you think that? I mean how can you be sure? Did you see it fall out of the cook's pocket?" Sergeant Wilder asked, looking worried. His keen mind suddenly went back to the casual chat with Betsy in the kitchen, and her claim that she had seen someone of that description in the back garden. The only other person that he knew who resembled him somewhat was Burt.

"Well, that rogue Burt is her son, isn't he? Unless of course, he was blackmailing someone else in this house. Wouldn't put anything past a criminal like that. Anyhow, I told Charles and Dennis about it as soon as I found it," Lydia said, looking smug at having caused a sensation.

"Do you have the note?" the inspector asked.

"I gave it to Dennis, so he's probably got it. You can check with him if you don't believe me!" Lydia Holden said.

"I don't doubt your word for a minute, Mrs. Holden. Just that this note is a serious piece of evidence and may shed some light on the events that took place last night. What time was this? That is, what time did you show the note to Lord Rutherford and Mr. Hawthorne?"

"Let me see. It must have been about 7:15. They were still working in the study together when I took it to them," Lydia replied, thinking back.

"And what was Mr. Hawthorne and Lord Rutherford's reaction to it?" the inspector asked.

"Well, Dennis said something about going to the summerhouse to check if this Burt character was still hanging about and, more importantly, who he was supposed to meet. And I told Charles to take a look in his safe in the study to make sure if the money he had placed there, the day before, was still there!" Lydia replied.

"Money? Was it a large sum?" the inspector asked.

"Yes, it must've been close to *five thousand pounds, Inspector*. Now I can't be sure since I didn't actually ask Charles how much it was or count the money myself, but that's a rough idea judging from the size of the bundles I saw. I remember thinking that one could buy a cottage or two and be set up for life, in these parts with that kind of money," Lydia replied matter-of-factly.

"Yes. Quite. And you saw Lord Rutherford place it in the safe?" Jeremy asked.

"No. I didn't actually see him place it there, Mr. Richards, but *I distinctly remember telling him to do so* after I saw the bundles lying in the desk drawer, when Charles opened it to give me some stamps two days ago. I also remember telling him that he ought not to keep so much money just lying about, especially when we have people related to criminals working here!" Lydia said in an insinuating manner, and added, "It's a wonder that *we haven't all been murdered in our beds yet* with that sort of cash kept around the place as if it were loose change!" she concluded.

"Er...yes, I rather agree with you there, Mrs. Holden. Leaving such large sums of money in easily accessible places is quite a careless thing to do, especially because it tends to breed temptation even in ordinarily honest people. By the way, did Lord Rutherford happen to tell you what or whom the money was meant for?" Inspector Parker asked hopefully.

"No Inspector. You may not be aware of this, but I am not the nosy kind. And I am definitely not one to take undue interest in my son-in-law's financial dealings," Lydia said, looking quite prim.

Sure and the 'Pope isn't Catholic,' was the silent, uncharitable thought that ran through Inspector Parker's mind. *I'll eat my hat if she doesn't know exactly how much he's worth, down to the last penny.*

"If I were you Inspector, I would concentrate more on gathering important facts such as this, rather than muddling about with the servant's hall gossip. And your next plan of action ought to be talking to Mr. Dennis Hawthorne as soon as possible. I'll send him to you right now," Lydia said as she walked out of the library with a righteous air about her.

"Charming woman," Jeremy said sardonically, after she left the room.

"Yes she's quite a piece of work! But surprisingly intelligent. Doesn't miss much, I'd say," said Inspector Parker, looking reflective.

Chapter Twelve

As Inspector Parker, Sergeant Wilder and Jeremy waited for Dennis Hawthorne in the library, Celia came down the stairs. She was still a little groggy from the medication that the nurse had given her according to Dr. Devine's instructions, but she managed to walk down by herself, holding the carved wooden banisters on the winding staircase into the main hall. The nurse had gone down late to get herself some mid-morning tea. Celia had gotten out of bed and dressed hurriedly. She had managed to throw on a simple grey wool sheath dress and brushed her hair. *I must speak to the police. I must speak to someone...tell them what I saw last night before I go mad.*

She stood still behind the pillar at the curve of the staircase as she saw her mother come out of the library and walk towards the study. The study door opened, and she could hear the sound of the typewriter in staccato bursts until the door closed behind Lydia. She thought quickly, *if Dennis was at work in the study, the police must be in the library.* This was her chance. She managed the last few steps and entered the library.

The three men got up from their arm chairs as she entered and closed the door behind her. Without wasting any time on niceties, she said to them, "I have to speak to you. I need to tell you all something. Look, I haven't much time before they... Mother finds out I'm here. What I'm going to tell you may seem mad... absolutely mad, but you must believe me. Really you must! I need your help."

They all stood staring at her.

"Please take a seat, Lady Celia," Jeremy spoke, the first one to come out of silence as recognition dawned.

"You know who I am?" she asked him with a puzzled look.

"Yes. You probably won't recognize me because you fell unconscious right after my car hit you last night on the driveway," he told her.

"No. I don't remember. But you are the police, aren't you?" she asked, looking puzzled once more.

"In a manner of speaking. My name is Jeremy Richards, and I used to be a detective at Scotland Yard... never mind. I was invited to your home last night for dinner by your husband. But I didn't get to meet him last night. You probably know that he is missing and Inspector Parker and Sergeant Wilder here are investigating the matter of his disappearance," Jeremy said, introducing the policemen.

"But that's just it. That's what I came to tell you. Charles hasn't disappeared. He was murdered. I saw him...lying there dead...and there was this knife in him, and I tried to help, and there was so much blood... it was horrible...and he was there...the killer...he came after me as well... I don't remember much after that. All I can remember is that the man who killed Charles was coming back for me, and I panicked and ran!" Celia spoke quickly and breathlessly and would have continued in the same vein, but Inspector Parker intervened at this point.

"Lady Celia, please, go slow. It's all very confusing. I understand you've had a shock, but let's take it one step at a time. You saw your husband lying dead. Where?" he asked her.

"In the study of course!" she replied.

"You are definite you saw your husband dead?" Jeremy asked her, just to make sure if she actually saw the body.

"Yes, I tell you he was dead. Stabbed to the heart. I knelt down and touched him and there was this dagger like thing still in him," she said.

"Did you touch it...the dagger?" Jeremy asked, suddenly alert.

"Yes, I think I tried to take it out... My mind was not working... All I could think of was that the thing had hurt him so badly and I wanted to get it out of his chest. Oh, I don't know why. He was already dead. My poor, poor Charles," she said, starting to sob.

"That explains the blood," Jeremy Richards said out loud and then thought to himself, *And there goes any chance of getting fingerprints of the perpetrator as well.*

Her fingerprints will be all over the murder weapon. Unless, of course, she killed him. She's either extremely clever or extremely stupid!

"Yes. There was so much blood. And it was still warm...ugh...and the French windows were wide open and flapping in the wind. The window banged, and I remember dropping that awful dagger-like thing. And I walked towards them to close them, and there was someone outside at a distance, so I stepped out to get a closer look... I felt someone was watching me... It was so dark and cold... and there was fog... I took a few more steps... The light from the windows didn't reach his face, so I couldn't make out his face...but I saw him. He was tall and had a great big overcoat. About the sergeant's height and build. And then he saw me, and started coming towards me. Charles was lying dead behind me. It was terrifying. I panicked and ran in the opposite direction," she told them between sobs.

"Towards the driveway?" Inspector Parker asked her.

"Yes, I think it must've been towards the driveway. Oh, it was all so horrible. And the worst part is, I can't remember what happened after that," she said, her eyes sending out an appeal for help towards Jeremy.

"You've had quite an ordeal Lady Celia. Perhaps a glass of water might help you calm down," Jeremy said , as he poured out some water from the carafe on the table in front of him and walked over to hand it to her.

"Thank you," she said to Jeremy as her sobs receded, and she felt herself calming down after taking a sip of water. *He looks like he believes me anyhow,* she thought to herself.

"But if you saw his body in the study and then ran out, then someone must've moved him afterwards," Sergeant Wilder said, looking puzzled.

"Could've been the killer Lady Celia saw," Jeremy said to him.

"Yes, but why? Why move the body? And where did he move it to?" Inspector Parker asked contemplatively.

"And why was there no sign of blood in the study or on the floor?" Sergeant Wilder added.

At that moment, the library doors opened and Lydia Holden walked in, followed by Dennis Hawthorne. Lydia started to speak to the inspector as she walked in, "Here's Mr. Hawthorne, and he will confirm what I just told..." Then she saw Celia seated in the armchair and stopped midway to address her in a sharp voice, "Celia! What are you doing here? You were given instructions to stay in bed. You are not well. You have no business to be here."

"Oh, Mother, stop it! I had to tell them what I saw last night!" Celia replied, her eyes watering up once more.

"You mean what you *imagined you saw.* Inspector, she is not in her senses. My daughter is prone to imagining things in the best of circumstances, and its better if you don't take anything she just told you seriously. She was given heavy medication last night and I'm afraid..." Lydia said, but her speech was cut short by the inspector before she could finish.

"Mrs. Holden, I'd request you to stop interfering with police business. Your daughter is very much in her senses and has just given us a very important statement that changes the very nature of this investigation."

"What do you mean?" Dennis asked the inspector.

"I mean, with the information Lady Celia has been kind enough to share with us, the matter of Lord Rutherford's disappearance has now become a full blown murder investigation," he told Dennis matter-of-factly.

II

The lunch gong had sounded. Lady Celia was escorted out of the room by her mother. Dennis asked Inspector Parker and Jeremy if they would be joining the family for lunch. They informed him that they would join them in about ten minutes. Dennis nodded and excused himself from the library, leaving Inspector Parker, Jeremy Richards and Sergeant Wilder to take stock of the new development in the case.

"Lady Celia's revelation has opened up a whole new can of worms! We had better get the Hopworths in for questioning immediately and find out about their son, Burt's whereabouts. That note Mrs. Holden mentioned may have something to do with all of this," Inspector Parker said to Sergeant Wilder.

"Surely, you don't think Burt had anything to do with this murder, Inspector!" Sergeant Wilder blurted out, unable to stop himself.

"Sergeant, this is a murder investigation now, and I'd require you to be as impersonal as you can, or I'll be forced to assign someone else to do the job if you don't feel up to investigating this case further," Inspector Parker said, a touch of steel creeping into his voice.

"No, Sir. I spoke out of line. You can be sure I will do what is required of me," Sergeant Wilder replied, regaining his professional tone once more. "And I will also ask Betsy the parlourmaid to give a formal statement. You see, a while ago, she may have let out that she saw Burt or someone of that description in the back garden last evening, just before the dinner party started."

"Good gracious! The case seems to be getting clearer by the minute. Perhaps you can ask the Hopworths to step in for questioning post lunch. And while you're at it, please ask Lady Elizabeth or Major Markham to call in the family solicitor. He will, in all probability, have the combination to the safe. We'd better check if the five thousand pounds are still there before we jump to any conclusions. Murders have been committed for less than one tenth the sum involved here," Inspector Parker said with a sigh.

"If money was the motivating factor here, I'd dare say you were right Inspector. In case the money is found to be missing, may I suggest that you call in the rest of your team that are currently searching the grounds and the woods to be re-assigned to conduct an immediate and thorough search within the house, especially the family, guest rooms and the servants' quarters," Jeremy said.

"You're quite right. Time is of the essence. It's still under twenty-four hours that the crime took place. We may still find some evidence. We'd best get to it Sergeant." Inspector Parker motioned to Sergeant Wilder as he picked up the phone in the library to put a call through to the station to ask for additional constables to aid in the search.

"It would also be a good idea if we found out from the solicitor who the direct beneficiaries of Lord Rutherford's will are," Jeremy said, speaking to Sergeant Wilder.

"You both think this is an inside job, don't you?" Sergeant Wilder asked as he made for the door.

"We can't rule out any possibilities at this point, Sergeant," Jeremy said, answering his query as Inspector Parker got busy on the phone.

Sergeant Wilder stopped as he reached the library door, waited a few moments for Inspector Parker to complete his call, and said, "Well, we do have a partial description of the killer from Lady Celia and then we need to check if there's anything in Betsy's story. I'm going to ask around in the village if any strangers of that description had been seen at the train station, pub or the inn last night."

"A good idea!" Inspector Parker said, putting down the receiver as he ended the quick call to the station.

"Hang on a moment Sergeant. It wasn't really much of a description...tall with a big coat! Good luck, trying to find our murderer with that! But before you go, there is something that I'd like to add that may actually help you zero in on whoever did this. You both do realise that if Lord Rutherford has in fact been murdered, you are up against an extremely audacious killer who managed to do the deed with a house full of guests and family," Jeremy said to them.

"Apart from being audacious, he also seems to be some sort of a magician. He whisked away the body of a full grown man after the deed, without leaving a trace. No bloodspots, no drag marks to the driveway, assuming of course, the body was driven away in a car. Given the amount of blood involved, it's downright puzzling," Inspector Parker mused.

"And with all the cars going and coming to the hall for the party, it's a wonder no one noticed when or how the body was carted away. One of the guest cars could have been used. I had better check each car that was here last night for traces," Sergeant Wilder said, reasserting his professional side.

"But it also looks as though someone here, in the house, must've helped him clean up the mess afterwards. It is beginning to look as though more than one person may have been involved in this crime," Inspector Parker said, thinking out loud.

He suspects Gladys, and Burt for sure, was the dominant thought that ran through Sergeant Wilder's mind as he heard the inspector's last statement.

As if reading his mind, the inspector said, "You did mention that the cook Gladys had been unusually reserved about her son Burt when you had questioned her about his whereabouts in the morning – seems to me that she may be concealing something."

"Yes, but murder? I'm not so sure about that," Sergeant Wilder mused and continued, "Sir, with all due respect, I am aware that mothers have been known to be protective of their children, but to go so far as to cover up a murder?! I don't know that Mrs. Hopworth or Burt would be capable of such a thing!"Sergeant Wilder said.

"We can't rule out any possibility at this point. We'll know more once the body turns up. It's bound to. We will need to be thorough," was Inspector Parker's response.

Jeremy spoke up, "You are right. In my experience with criminal psychological profiling, I would consider this person or persons to be extremely intelligent but also with an arrogance bordering on megalomania, which will in all likelihood trip them up in the end. I have come across several such cases and killers before at Scotland Yard *and I have caught them every single time."*

He's not very far from being a megalomaniac himself, thought Sergeant Wilder, as he looked contemplatively at Jeremy Richards before he finally left the library.

Chapter Thirteen

"I say, Suzie, something's not right here!" Betsy said, looking confused. She was helping Suzie clear the lunch things after the family had left the dining room.

"About what?" Suzie asked.

"You know, I met Cindy at the village a few months back and we got talking. She was all excited about something, and I thought it was because she was all excited about steppin' out with the sergeant. And I was pulling the sergeant's leg about it when he was speaking to Mrs. Hopworth, but now I don't know."

"Know what? Some girls get excited over silly things like that," Suzie responded.

"Yes, but the sergeant said Cindy had dumped him right after the dance...and just before lunch Henry came to deliver the post and he asked me if I'd heard that Cindy had left the village. All packed up and left! Not a word to anyone. And he said he was going to miss her, seeing as she's quit her job at the pub and gone off somewhere...like on a trip or something."

"Now, that is strange. Wonder where she's off to without a word to anyone? Probably some man or other. Girls like that always get into trouble...a red head like that. I say, wasn't she engaged to Mrs. Hopworth's son before he got into all that trouble?" Suzie asked, as a flash of memory struck her.

"Yes, but that was ages ago. She dropped poor Burt like a hot potato after the sentencing. There was talk about her mooning over Sergeant Wilder soon after that. Ambitious little thing like her...I wouldn't be surprised if she's thrown him over now to run off with someone with a bit more dosh!" Betsy said acidly.

"Oh well, girls like Cindy usually come to a bad end. She always did have the knack for choosing the bad 'uns. I'd say the good sergeant was well out of it!" Suzie said, moralizing.

"Yes. I suppose you're right. And another thing. I overheard Lady Celia telling her mother in the morning that she thought she had seen Sir Charles murdered in the study last evening before her accident!"

"What? Murdered? How horrible! In the study, you say? But where's the body then? It can't be. She must've had a bad dream after getting knocked by that car and all."

"That's what Queen Mary told her, but I don't know... There's been some strange going on's here, I can tell you that! And there was something else I meant to ask you. What was it now? I am gettin' so muddle headed these days. Yes...the white sheepskin rug is missing from the study. You know the furry one near the big writing table? Do you know if anyone took it out to be aired or cleaned?" Betsy asked Suzie in a puzzled tone, as she joined her in the pantry.

"No, but I'll look out for it. Perhaps Queen Mary had it removed by one of the boys. I'll ask around. But that's not the only thing missing, you know. Mr. Hawthorne's fancy ivory handle paper cutter is gone as well. The one with all the squiggly carvings of elephants and tigers and what not on it. He asked me this morning, if I had seen it anywhere and I said I'd search for it while cleaning. So if you find it anywhere, let me know. He says it's his lucky charm, and he's had it since he was a boy in India. I asked him if it was very precious, and he said, 'Not really, but I'd like it back - so let's pretend that some Maharajah gave it to me.' Likely story, I thought to myself! But he can be funny when he's not all serious and broody, that one," Suzie said with a smile.

"Right! It's probably lying about under those piles of books in the study somewhere. That place is a right mess, it is. Anyhow, I'll get to it later. Best get on with our work for now. Mrs. Hopworth has just gone to the library with Sergeant Wilder and left me to put the cakes in the oven for the evening tea," Betsy said, making a face.

II

"I was wondering if you could explain this note from your son, Mrs. Hopworth?" Inspector Parker asked Gladys as soon as she entered the library. His tactic was to give a suspect no time to think, and he had found in his years of experience that the element of surprise, in such situations often brought out the truth with amazing speed.

"I well...Sir...where did you find it?" Gladys replied, flustered, as Mr. Hopworth and the others looked on.

At this point Hopworth took a step forward and asked, "Might I take a look at it? If you don't mind, Sir."

"Not at all. Here you are," Inspector Parker replied, handing the piece of paper over to him.

Hopworth read the few lines on it quickly, and with his face set in stone, turned to ask his wife in a low voice, "What is the meaning of all this, Gladys?"

When he got no reply, he asked her again, in a grim voice "Gladys, has that rogue been here?"

At this, Mrs. Hopworth looked up with teary eyes, "Oh John, don't call him that. He is our son. Our own flesh and blood."

"He is no son of mine!" Hopworth roared at her with an uncharacteristic display of anger.

Inspector Parker was taken aback. "Now there, Hopworth. It will do no good to anybody here to lose your temper. Control yourself man."

"I'm very sorry, Sir," Hopworth said, making a herculean effort to regain his placidity. And continued, "I hope you will forgive my outburst, but I had expressly forbidden that boy to come back here ever again to meet me or my wife, and now I find that my own wife is not to be trusted."

Gladys spoke up through her tears, "My boy has nothing to do with any of this Inspector. He made a mistake once, and he's done his time and more. Now he's got a chance to start a new life and wanted some help from me, that's all."

"What sort of help?" the inspector asked her in a gentle voice.

"Well, you see Sir, a friend of his at that London hotel he worked in, told him he could get him a job as an overseer in a new coffee plantation somewhere in East Africa – some place called Kenya. Burt just needed some extra money to pay for the passage to Africa and the rest of the journey by road to reach the estate in Kenya. It was a chance of a lifetime for him, and I had to help, you see... My boy has no one else to turn to, now that his own father has disowned him," Gladys replied, sniffling into her handkerchief and throwing a bitter glance at Hopworth.

"How much money did he need, Mrs. Hopworth?" Jeremy asked politely, entering the conversation.

"A hundred pounds Sir," she replied with dignity.

"Where would you get a hundred quid to give him?" Hopworth interjected, with a puzzled look on his face.

"Well, if you must know John, I gave him our savings and sold my pearl earrings and the bracelet you bought me," Gladys replied tartly.

"What! All of our life's savings and all your jewellery! I saved up for years and years for those!" Hopworth said, his anger returning.

"And what good is money or fancy jewels to me if I can't help my only son start a new life?" Gladys said, raising her own voice, looking at him. Hopworth sighed and put his hand to his brows, shaking his head sadly. Gladys continued in a gentler voice. "John, think what it means for Burt to have a proper job again. He's been so miserable the past few years doing dirty dishes and awful jobs that common dustmen wouldn't touch. Our only son! Oh, John, think how different it will all be now for him - an overseer of a big coffee estate!"

"I'm afraid that can't happen just yet, Mrs. Hopworth. Since he was on the grounds at or around the time of the murder, he is a suspect in this investigation and, as such, will not be allowed to leave the country until this matter is cleared up," Inspector Parker told her.

"But Sir, he had nothing to do with all of this. He only came here because I told him I had the money ready for him. And if he can't get on the ship now, he may lose this chance of a job forever!"

"The law is the law and I'm afraid it must be obeyed. We have to have him brought back here for further questioning. Would you happen to know which ship he has booked his passage for?" the inspector queried.

She hesitated but spoke up under the inspector's direct, uncompromising gaze, "He mentioned something about taking an ocean liner out of Southampton...Carnival Castle...or something like that, but I may have got the name wrong. It sounded something like that, anyhow. It's supposed to sail for a place called Mombasa in Africa this Wednesday."

"Right. That doesn't give us much time. We'll wire Southampton immediately and try to locate him and get him here for questioning. Sergeant, can you get on it now?" Inspector Parker asked.

"On my way now, Sir," was Sergeant Wilder's grim faced response as he made his way to the door.

"Oh, but Sir, it would ruin his chances forever. Have a heart, Sir! He had nothing to do with all of this," Gladys made one last appeal, before bursting into tears.

Hopworth intervened with a sigh, "Come now, Gladys. The police are right. They have to get him here for questioning if he was here that night. It's no good fighting the law."

"Please, Mrs. Hopworth. We need you to calm down. If he is innocent, I'm sure there will be other chances for your son. Now, can you tell me exactly when and where you met Burt and how long did your meeting last on the night in question?" Inspector Parker asked her.

Gladys stopped sniffling and replied in a small voice, "Well Sir, seeing as it was the night of the party, I had a lot of things to do. My mind was on so many things at the time, there was a mishap...the soufflé had been burnt, and I had to rummage up an apple crumble for dessert last minute instead. So I got delayed. I was supposed to meet Burt at seven, but he had to wait a while till I could get the pie in the oven, and then I took the money with me and went to meet him at the summerhouse."

"What time would that have been?" Inspector Parker asked her.

"About 7:15, I think, Sir. Perhaps it was 7:20. I can't be sure because I remember now, it took me another five minutes to set the hors d'oeuvres on trays in the pantry and instruct Suzie in the order they were supposed to be served," she replied, sounding unsure.

"Right, and then you headed towards the summer house?" He asked.

"Yes, Sir," she said.

"And that would have taken you another ten minutes, I suppose?"

"Not quite, Sir. You see, Burt waited at the summerhouse for me, and then seeing as I had not come there, he thought that I had not gotten his note so he started walking towards the kitchen hoping to spot me there. And as it were such a foggy night, he hoped he wouldn't be seen by anyone else. I nearly didn't see him myself, till I almost walked into him, Sir," she told the inspector.

"Where was that?" Jeremy asked her, suddenly alert to a different possibility.

"About half way to the summerhouse, Sir, through the grounds. Near the big cedar. I could just about make it out through the fog when I handed him the money."

"Can you show us the spot Mrs. Hopworth?" The inspector asked, picking up on Jeremy's line of thought.

"Yes, Sir," she said hesitantly, her mother's instinct telling her that these men were trying to get at something that she was unaware of, and might get Burt into further trouble. But her better sense prevailed and she said, "If you would like to see it now, Sir..."

Both Jeremy Richards and Inspector Parker started heading towards the French windows. Inspector Parker stopped to wave his hand motioning her to lead the way and said, "Right, Let's get going. After you, Mrs. Hopworth."

They walked out through the French windows onto the lawn, and Mrs. Hopworth started towards the big cedar they could see in the distance.

Jeremy Richards made a quick mental calculation that it was about fifteen hundred yards from the library and study windows, and it would have been impossible for Burt to have seen what was going on inside the study from that distance, especially with the deep fog that had surrounded the countryside that night. *Unless Burt had deliberately walked towards the study windows under that curtain of fog with a different intent. It could have been him Lady Celia had seen at a distance in the fog.* But until they knew for sure that the money was missing, Burt had to be given the benefit of doubt. Minus the money angle, Burt's motive to kill Sir Charles was blurred at best.

But Jeremy had a thought that also ran through the Inspector's head. Even if Burt had nothing to do with the murder, there was a distinct possibility that he might have seen or heard something on the night of the murder. *Burt must be found and brought in for questioning,* was the uppermost thought that ran through both their minds.

Chapter Fourteen

Dennis was on his way downstairs as Celia was on her way up to her room to fetch her wrap.

He stopped her midway, on the landing and said, "Celia, I need to speak with you."

"Not now Dennis. I can't talk. There is just too much going on. Besides, I need to be back downstairs in a moment. The inspector needs me," Celia said with a touch of impatience, as she walked past him, continuing up the stairs.

He caught her arm to stop her and she turned back to face him with an alarmed expression on her face. "What are you doing, Dennis? Let me go!" she said in an angry voice. Suzie, who had been dusting the marble table in the hallway below, stopped to glance up at the stairwell.

Dennis noticed the parlourmaid staring at them and lowered his voice and said, "Alright. But I have to talk to you, my darling. I must. We need to discuss what happened that night."

"There is nothing to discuss! Now please, if you don't mind..." she said to him coldly, wrenching her hand out of his grip.

He let her go. He could see that Suzie was keeping an eye on them and under the circumstances, it was best that he meet Celia privately. He came down the remainder of the stairs nonchalantly, and giving Suzie a friendly nod, addressed her, "Any sign of my elusive ivory paper knife, Suzie?"

"Not yet, Sir, but I've informed Betsy to keep an eye out for it aswell. It's sure to turn up, Sir. I'll bring it to you as soon as we find it."

"Thank you my dear girl. What would I do without you?" he said in a flirty voice, and Suzie blushed.

"I'm sure you'll be fine, Sir. If you'll excuse me now, Sir, I need to go and get the fires started in the study and the library," she said, edging backwards.

"Work before worship and all that sort of thing, eh? Go on then," he said to her playfully, enjoying her embarrassment.

"Yes, Sir. Thank you, Sir," Suzie said, as she turned and quickened her pace towards the baize door that led to the servant's hall.

That'll give her something to talk about other than Celia and me, Dennis smiled to himself. Everything was going just as he had planned. If only he could get Celia to see, how clever he really had been, in covering their tracks!

II

They were all having afternoon tea in the sitting room, discussing various possibilities related to the case. The thorough search the police had carried out through the rooms in the hall, including the servant's quarters had yielded nothing. The discussion moved to finding the combination for the safe in the study.

"Oh! I can help you with that. I know the combination. Charles showed me so I could put my jewels in and take them out as I needed them," Lady Celia said casually, taking a sip of tea.

This statement startled everyone, as Major Markham had just finished informing them that the safe could not be opened until the solicitors came down with the combination. He also told them that he had been informed by the firm that their representative could only join them two days later with the combination of the safe.

"Well, my dear! Why didn't you say anything about it before? James and I have been desperately trying to contact the solicitors to get that safe opened for the police," Elizabeth Markham asked Celia.

"No one asked me. How was I to know you needed the combination?" was her simple response.

After tea, Celia and the others were joined by the inspector in the study. She walked up to the painting by Albert Bierstadt of cows grazing on a windswept hill and pushed the frame. The painting swung open on hinges hidden in the panelled oak of the study. As the safe came into view, she deftly turned the knobs, and the heavy door of the safe opened noiselessly. She moved aside from the open safe to give Inspector Parker access to it. He craned his neck to check its contents. His trained eye quickly took a measure of what was in it. He double checked and saw that there were some legal documents, land leases, some boxes and velvet pouches with jewellers' logos on them, share certificates and a pile of Government bonds, but no bundles of money.

"There's no sign of any money in here," the inspector said, turning to look at Lady Celia and the others.

"Would you know, Lady Celia, why he had that sum of money in the house? Was he planning to invest in some venture?" he asked her.

"I did see him put the money in the desk and I remember at the time, he mentioned something about wanting to help someone start up their life again. And no, I don't know who he was referring to. Charles was a good man. It didn't surprise me at all, that he wanted to help someone," Celia said, with a melancholy smile.

III

Dusk had set in and the inspector was ready to pack up the investigation for the day, when Sergeant Wilder entered the study and addressed him, "Sir, we've just had a wire from Southampton, and they've located Burt Hopworth. He was due to sail for Mombasa on the Carnarvon Castle. He's being brought back for questioning as we speak."

"Excellent work, Sergeant! Now we should be able to get to the bottom of this," Inspector Parker said.

"It's not just that, Sir, but on a hunch, I asked them to check to see if he was travelling alone, and it turns out that there were in fact two passages booked in his name.

Mr. and a Mrs. Burt Hopworth. So far, we haven't found the mysterious Mrs. Burt, but the police at Southampton have questioned him about it. Apparently, Burt claimed that the Mrs. was supposed to meet him somewhere but hadn't shown up. Sounded a bit dodgy to me, so I've asked them to look into it. The Southampton police are trying to locate the woman in question."

"Well, that's an interesting bit of news. Any idea who this mystery woman is?" the inspector queried.

"No, Sir, but I'm sure we'll find out sooner than later!" Sergeant Wilder said confidently.

"That's a nifty bit of police work, Sergeant," Jeremy said to him with admiration.

"Thank you, Sir," was Sergeant Wilder's response.

IV

The Inspector and Jeremy were about to take their leave from the rest of the family. Everyone had gathered in the study for the latest update on the case, when Rachel Markham walked into the study with a book in her hands and said to Lady Celia, "I just had an idea. Celia, you said you found Uncle Charles' body over here. Now then, if I were a murderer and I wanted to hide the body for reasons of my own...possibly to buy more time so that I could move it later at an opportune moment..."

"Oh, Rachel, don't be gruesome! It's bad enough we have to deal with all this without your nonsensical ideas," Elizabeth Markham spoke, interrupting her flow.

"No, no. Do go on Rachel. What is it you thought of?" Jeremy asked her.

"Well..." she said haltingly, looking at the sea of disapproving faces, and then suddenly a change came over her, as if Jeremy's support had empowered her, and she continued, "You see, I've just been reading this book, and in it, the body is hidden in a secret enclosure or what is commonly known as a priest's hole. Now, this is also an old house, and I do remember Uncle Charles showing me a secret opening when I was a child. It was a smallish space, about four feet wide, behind a book shelf, but I remember it fascinated my imagination for days! But for the life of me, I can't remember where it was - here or in the library. I wonder if anyone's thought of looking in there?" she asked innocently.

Suddenly there was a buzz in the room and Jeremy said, "Thank you, Rachel. That's quite an eye opener. Wonder why we've all missed that possibility entirely. Inspector, I think she may have something there, if there is indeed a secret alcove somewhere here."

"Yes, indeed. But you say you can't remember where it was?" Inspector Parker asked.

"Oh, I've only been back here for about a year, but someone's bound to know. Someone who has been here longer. Hopworth for instance, or Dennis, what about you? You've been writing all those memoirs. Surely it may have come up somewhere? Uncle Charles used to joke about going 'underground' every time the Vicar's wife or some other village biddy came around to rattle on about some fete or the other. I assumed he hid in his secret hiding place, and no one could find him till the women went away!" she said, looking at Dennis.

"Yes. Yes...I think it was mentioned somewhere..." he faltered, "I'm not sure which year, but I'll look into it," he said, going through the stacks of paper lying on the desk next to the typewriter.

At that moment, Hopworth entered the study and addressed the inspector, "Sir, there is a telephone call from the station for you. If you would care to take it in the hall?"

"Oh bother! Tell them I'll call back," the inspector replied, and then, as Hopworth said "Very good, Sir" and turned to walk towards the door, the inspector stopped him. "Wait a moment, Hopworth. Would you happen to know the exact location of a certain secret hiding place in this room or the library? Like a priest's hole?"

"Yes Sir. It is right over there...behind this bookshelf near the door," Hopworth said, casually.

"My good man, why did you not share this information with us before!" Inspector Parker asked, baffled.

"My apologies, Sir, it did not occur to me," was Hopworth's reply.

"Never mind. Now Hopworth, would you happen to know where the secret lever that operates it is?" the inspector asked Hopworth as Rachel moved to investigate the bookshelf on the far end heavy with leather bound volumes of estate reports.

"I'm afraid Lord Rutherford did not share that information with me Sir. I did see him exiting from the space once, many years ago, and that is how I came to know of its existence," Hopworth said, matter-of-factly.

Rachel had started pulling out books from the upper right corner, as if a faint memory from childhood came back to her. When she tugged at the fifth book, the entire shelf moved like a door slowly swinging back on its hinges, soundlessly. She stepped back and gasped, "Oh! How awful!" And then faltered backwards as Jeremy reached her and held her steady. Her face had gone very white. Both Sergeant Wilder and the inspector reached the alcove.

"I'll go ring for the doctor and the coroner, Sir," Sergeant Wilder said grimly, as everyone else came forward out of a natural curiosity to see what Rachel had seen. Sir Charles' body was huddled in a sitting position. He was partially wrapped in a white rug stained with dried blood. His eyes were open, with a look of terror in them, and his fists were clenched unnaturally in front of him in an advanced state of rigor mortis.

The inspector became rigid, and with an air of authority, turned to address the group of people in the study, "I think it is safe to assume that Lord Rutherford's body has been found. I would request everyone to leave the room, please. Lady Elizabeth, I would request you to keep this room locked for the night after the body is removed. This room will now be off limits until the forensic team finishes their work. I hope I can expect your full cooperation in this."

Elizabeth Markham was the first to regain her composure and said, "You can be assured of that, Inspector." Then she put her arms around Rachel's shoulders and in an uncharacteristic display of maternal warmth, she said gently, "Come, my dear. There's nothing more for you to do here."

As mother and daughter left the room, the others followed suit. Celia was weeping silently as Dennis and Lydia both came forward to escort her out.

Chapter Fifteen

The body had been taken for examination, and the police were collecting material evidence and dusting the study and the alcove for fingerprints.

Night had set in, and Jeremy had joined Rachel for a walk. It was a mild and clear winter night, and there was a full moon lighting up the night sky. Under different circumstances, it would have been a perfect setting for a romantic walk.

Rachel was angry. It was the first time in her life she was experiencing a cold, dark anger from deep within. "Uncle Charles was a good man and a decent human being. He didn't deserve this," she told him in a calm and controlled voice that belied the emotions raging within her.

Jeremy walked quietly beside her. He could sense the deep wave of shock and anger that had engulfed her when she had found the body. He understood it.

Rachel continued, "You know Jeremy, it wasn't real to me. None of it was real... Until I saw what someone had done to him. This whole thing was unreal up until then. It was more like I was living in one of my fast-paced mystery books, and there was some excitement about all that was happening. The sadness of it was not real. The indignity! I will never ever be able to forget that awful hunted look in his eyes. He didn't deserve to be put to death like this. I am going to find out whoever did this to him, and I will not rest until justice is served."

They walked a few more paces in complete silence towards the woods. Then Rachel turned towards him, leaned forward, and gave him a peck on the cheek and said, "Thank you."

"For what? I haven't done anything. Yet..." was Jeremy's quiet response. He was touched by her faith in him.

"For just being there. For not judging me for how I was before. I can't imagine what I was thinking, the things I said. The way I behaved...like it was all a game...a silly mystery novel waiting to be solved. So bloody stupid and insensitive. I could kick myself," Rachel said, her eyes downcast.

He stopped her and put his arms on her shoulders and turned her towards him. Then, looking directly into her eyes, said, "Rachel, however you behaved, it was not a crime. There's no need to judge yourself so harshly. I'd mark it down to your natural, youthful exuberance and inexperience in such matters, if I were you. Besides, the real criminal is out there, smugly watching all of this with a false satisfaction that he or she has been rather clever.

If you really want to help the police solve this crime, I will share a trick with you that may help us to trap whoever did this."

"Yes, please. I would do anything you ask. I really want to help you and the police, Jeremy," Rachel said, as they entered the wooded area near the summerhouse.

"Right. Then, the very best thing you can do now for your Uncle Charles is to keep your wits about you and observe," Jeremy said.

"Observe what?" she asked, puzzled. It was getting darker as the trees got thicker, and the moonlight fell through the canopy of trees in pools of white light. She held his hand. The summerhouse came into view. There was something magical about it standing amidst the trees, moonlight reflecting off its glass panes. Rachel guided him towards it. Hand in hand she walked in with Jeremy. She felt strangely relaxed and protected, just having his masculine presence beside her. It was warmer inside, and it seemed natural to close the glass doors once they entered to shield them from the chill.

Jeremy continued speaking, "Everything and everyone. The things people let slip. Small things, often inadvertently revealed, tend to unravel larger things. If you are on the lookout for the truth, you will find it. Besides, you are in the comfortable position where people may say things in front of you that they wouldn't dream of talking about in front of us," he said, feeling good about her hand in his. It felt right somehow. After a long time, he had this strange sense of really being with a woman as they stood side by side looking out the windows of the summerhouse. He noticed her moonlit profile for the first time as they stared out of the partially frosted glass panes, and it brought him pleasure to realise that like her mother, she had almost perfect features but unlike her mother, she had a certain softness in them that appealed more to him. As if in the last few hours, she had transformed in his mind's eye from a childlike girl to a woman. A beautiful woman. A desirable woman.

"I see what you mean. It's safe for others to assume I'm a complete dolt, my behaviour up until now being proof of the pudding. Most people will probably not be on their guard, as they would in front of you or the police," she acquiesced, as she turned to face him.

"Precisely! So the best *modus operandi* would be for you to continue letting everyone think you are er...the same person you were before you discovered the body, and you may be surprised at what happens," he said, smiling faintly at how he had stopped himself just in time from using her own description of 'a dolt'. Of course, she was far from it. She was quite an intelligent and passionate girl, in her own indescribable way. A force to be reckoned with.

"Alright. I'll do it," was Rachel's determined response.

"Just a word of caution. We are dealing with an extremely ruthless killer here, so I want you to be careful. Trust no one. And never let your guard down for a moment. Most importantly, keep me informed about everything you see and hear so that I can look out for you aswell. I don't want anything happening to you, do you understand?" he told her sternly.

"Why?" she asked him, as she looked directly into his eyes with an impish smile.

"What do you mean, why? Of course, I don't want anything to happen to..." Jeremy started to say angrily, but Rachel came forward and covered his mouth with hers with an unexpected kiss.

As his initial shock at being suddenly kissed by her subsided, he found himself wanting more of her sweetness and pulled her towards him. Their lips came together again, his tongue found its way into her mouth. His mind was no longer his. She was like a strange cocktail of summer wine and heady perfume. His arms went around her as she started returning the passionate kiss with an exploration of her own. In the middle of it all, he found himself thinking... *This is wrong. She's too young for you. She's just a child with a woman's body.* He took his arms back, and she felt his withdrawal. She gently took his hands in hers, as if she could read his mind. Then, with deliberate slowness, as if it were the most natural thing in the world, she kissed him again, her eyes holding him captive under the moonlit panes.

As his mouth sought hers once more, his fingers explored further, and his logical mind deserted him completely. Their bodies started melting into each other. *Oh God, I must stop this...* In the midst of their passionate embrace she had somehow taken off his thick woollen overcoat, and he found himself being pulled down to the rug below, his body covering hers. Jeremy shifted her onto his overcoat, which was lying on the rug, and her fingers moved to his head, playing with his hair. Pleasure moved like waves in his body, and as she lay on her back, she brought her hands up behind his neck and pulled him into another mind numbingly sensual kiss. At this point, he moaned and lifted his head. Looking into her eyes, he said in a thick voice laden with desire, "Rachel let's stop now. Please. I'm losing control. I am not a saint."

She smiled back with humour in her smoky eyes and said softly, "Thank heavens for that. I want you Jeremy, now, before they find us frozen to death here."

He looked into her eyes and his clouded mind suddenly cleared to reality. "Rachel, no. It's all wrong. You don't realise what you're saying. You are in a state of shock. I don't want us to do anything you'll regret later. I'm old enough to be your..." he couldn't quite get himself to say father.

She sighed and said forlornly, "Damn! Rejected on my very first attempt to seduce the first man I really like! How sad for a girl..." her eyes began to fill up with unshed tears of humiliation.

"Come here, you vixen," he said playfully as he grabbed her and gave her a deep kiss. "I am not rejecting you, you silly, beautiful girl! Merely postponing your first experience with me to a better time and a more comfortable place. Do you understand?"

"Right. Now I feel worse. Like a tart. Sorry, didn't mean to throw myself at you. It just happened. But I'll live," she said, gritting her teeth.

"Goodness gracious! There isn't an ounce of 'tart' about you. You just happen to be the classiest and most fearless young lady I've ever met, with a brain to match. I would love to make you mine, if you still want me that is, in the clear light of day – make no mistake about that. But not," he said, pausing, waving his hand around the summerhouse, "here – in this haven of dust and cobwebs and not like this. You deserve better," he told her gravely, as they got up and adjusted their clothing. He dusted his coat before gently covering her, and he kissed her on the forehead, and then they headed back to the house together.

II

As Jeremy and Rachel entered the library through the French windows, Elizabeth Markham rose from her arm chair and addressed Rachel in a distressed tone, "Oh, darling, where were you? I was so worried." She came up and put her arms around her daughter.

"It's not like you to worry, Mums. What's happened?" Rachel asked her.

"Haven't you heard? No...of course not. The Inspector got a call from the station a few minutes ago. It seems the body of a young woman in her early twenties has just been found in the woods not far from here. The inspector and the sergeant just left. I couldn't find you anywhere in the house, and after what's happened to Charles. Oh! I didn't know what to think. Thank God you are safe!" Elizabeth Markham said, holding Rachel close to her.

"How awful for you, Mums. I'm sorry I didn't tell you I was going out for a walk. I was so upset after finding... you know...I just wanted to be out in the open for a while, and anyway Jeremy was with me, so there was nothing to worry about. I'm feeling much better now," Rachel said, looking over her mother's shoulder and giving Jeremy a naughty smile. He blushed.

Jeremy spoke up, "Er...ah ladies, I think I had better go to the station." He felt like a school boy. He had to get away from her mother's scrutiny. Then he remembered the woman's body being found in the woods and, regaining his professional air, asked, "Where is Lady Celia? Is she in the house?"

Lady Elizabeth answered "Oh, yes. Celia is up in her room. Detective, please find out what is going on. This used to be such a safe haven, and now all these deaths. It's simply terrifying to think that one is not safe, even in one's home, anymore."

"Lady Elizabeth, I understand your fears. We don't know as yet if the two deaths are connected in any way. I'll find out what I can and keep you posted. Meanwhile, I'd advise you to instruct your staff to keep the French windows locked and the house secure at all times until we find out who is behind all this," Jeremy told her before leaving the room, not giving voice to the nagging thought in his head that the killer could well be a member of their household.

Rachel escorted him out the main door as her mother went to ask Hopworth to do the needful and secure the house. Once they were out of viewing distance, he turned to Rachel and said, "Bye now, love. Stay safe, keep your door locked at night and I'll see you tomorrow." He left after giving her a peck on her lips.

Chapter Sixteen

After Jeremy left Rutherford Hall, he drove straight to the village main street and parked near the police station. It was almost nine at night, and lights shone out of the windows of the unassuming red brick structure, which was a complete antithesis of the imposing structure of Scotland Yard. The rustic rural station even had a trellis-covered entrance and a porch with potted flowers and window boxes with carnations and mini chrysanthemums in bloom.

He made his way through the crowd of people mulling about outside. In a sleepy village like this, petty thefts and small crimes were infrequent. It was only natural that a second body being found in such close succession had caused quite a sensation.

"Have a seat, Detective Richards," Inspector Parker motioned towards a chair in his cubicle at the police station. He looked tired.

"Thank you. I came as soon as I heard. That's quite a crowd outside the station," Jeremy said, as he lowered himself onto the wooden seat.

"Yes. Terrible business, all this. Starting tomorrow, the newspapers are going to have a field day. I'll probably have to appoint some of my men just to keep sensation hunters at bay," Inspector Parker grimaced.

"Yes, I can imagine. We always lost the battle against the tabloids up at the Yard. That said, they do sometimes help in garnering information and getting the public involved in tracking down suspects that elude us. So it's never a total loss. Have you identified the body yet?" Jeremy asked.

"Yes. The body of the young woman has been positively identified as Miss Cindy Jones. She used to work as a barmaid at the local village pub, 'The Golden Goose.' We won't know the time of death exactly until the autopsy is done, but the doctor mentioned that it could be anywhere between twenty-four to thirty-six hours, putting it very close to the time that Lord Rutherford was reported missing," the inspector said.

"In other words, the timing is too close for comfort, and the body was found too close to Rutherford Hall to be written off as a coincidence," Jeremy mused.

"Quite."

"So you do think the two deaths are connected?"

"In a nutshell, there is a high possibility that may be the case, and that we have a serial strangler on the loose," Inspector Parker said, leaning towards him across the table.

"A strangler? But I understood that Lord Rutherford was stabbed to death," Jeremy said.

"The doctor who examined the body says otherwise. It was true that he had been stabbed multiple times, by what we have now identified as Mr. Dennis Hawthorne's oriental paper cutting knife, and bled quite a bit as one of the arteries was cut...but the actual cause of death was strangulation by a pair of very strong hands. The vertebrae in the neck were broken. Very similar to the way Miss Jones' neck was broken. We'll know for sure if they shared the same killer once the coroner's report comes in," Inspector Parker said.

"Good Lord! A double hit. Seems like more than one person wanted to make sure that Lord Rutherford was out of the way," Jeremy said, one eyebrow raised.

"Yes, it's downright puzzling! An easy-going, affable man like that with no known enemies. It's difficult enough to try and figure out who would have a motive. I hoped we'd know more once Burt Hopworth got here, but now it seems like there's more than one person involved...where is the motive, Detective Richards?" asked Inspector Parker, bewilderment written all over his face.

Jeremy said, "Well, to my mind, Inspector, there seems to be motives galore for you to choose from. Apart from the Burt Hopworth angle, what about the Lord's impoverished sister and brother-in-law who would inherit a good deal of his money? After all, it can't be much fun living on hand-outs."

"But they seem to have rock solid alibis for the time of the murder!" the inspector interjected.

"Yes, conveniently provided by one another. Perhaps with a bit of scratching on the surface, the alibis may not be as rock solid as we may think. Then of course, there's the scheming mother-in-law whose own husband died under mysterious circumstances in India," Jeremy said.

"Eh, what?" Inspector Parker interjected.

"Apparently, Mr. Holden died in a mysterious fire in his tea factory in India, which, to my mind, could have been arson by someone who wanted to kill him," Jeremy explained.

"But why would she want to kill her husband?" the inspector asked.

"There could be a hundred reasons. You know, Inspector, statistics show us that close to ninety percent of all murders are usually committed by a spouse," was Jeremy's response.

"Yes. But even so, what's her motive to get her son-in-law out of the way?" he asked.

"The threat of losing a comfortable position as chatelaine of a large household sounds like motive enough to me, for a woman who obviously relishes being in control. Look at the alternative for her if she were to be asked to leave his house. What was it that Lady Celia had said... Yes, I quote, 'the two penny quarters you could afford...' There's your motive," Jeremy reminded him.

"Hmm. I didn't think of that. Although, it still sounds a bit farfetched to me, I'll admit. I can't picture her as much of a strangler...a poisoner, perhaps, but the strangling is definitely a man's job."

"Yes, I quite agree, but you are overlooking the fact that she could have had an accomplice. With a strong motive, anything is possible. The carrot can be dangled to get one's job done if the idea and the supporting intelligence are there, Inspector. And I would say that there is a good deal of intelligence there, wouldn't you?" Jeremy pointed out.

"Yes, you could be right. I mean, even someone like James Markham or that daughter of theirs could possibly be recruited as accomplices, if she gave them a nudge in the right direction. That Rachel girl seemed to zero in on the hiding place of the body pretty easily."

"But then, why would she, when she could've just stayed mum if she were involved and they could have had time to move the body to the woods or some other place?" he asked.

"To throw us off their scent, obviously!" the Inspector said.

"No, I don't believe the girl is involved in any way," Jeremy said emphatically.

"Getting a soft corner for her, are we?" the Inspector asked with a wink.

"Balderdash! I just don't think she had anything to do with it, quite simply because she went into a very real state of shock on finding her uncle's body. Besides, it appeared to me as though she was genuinely fond of her uncle," he said casually, his years of professional training covered up the way he felt about Rachel now. He was still walking on air after their passionate kissing session in the summerhouse. Whether it was a strong reaction to finding her uncle's body, or not, Rachel had made him feel young, energetic and virile once more. *If only the inspector knew how positively Rachel had gone into shock,* he thought, smiling inwardly.

Inspector Parker was no fool. He let it drop, seeing how protective Jeremy was being about her. And found himself thinking that either Jeremy could be right or Rachel Markham could possibly fall into the category of being a very clever and manipulative little actress. Trying to pick Jeremy's brains further, aloud, he said, "Any other possible angles on your mind?"

"Yes. The lovebirds for instance," Jeremy said without hesitation.

"You've lost me there completely, Detective," was the inspector's deadpan response.

"Dennis Hawthorne and Lady Celia. And Dennis Hawthorne's paper cutter used as a weapon, you say? If stabbing seems more like a woman's crime while strangling is most definitely something a man would do, these two ought to be your prime suspects. I'd bring both him and Lady Celia in for further questioning, if I were you," Jeremy prompted.

"Yes, we've already got Dennis Hawthorne here at the Station for an interview. But what's the connection between him and Lady Celia?" the inspector asked, puzzled.

"You do know they had a history together - Mr. Hawthorne and Lady Celia?" Jeremy asked the inspector.

"I was not aware of that! You mean a romantic involvement?" the inspector asked, his eyes lighting up with interest.

"Yes. I have it from the horse's mouth — Mr. Hawthorne himself. Apparently, they were long lost childhood sweethearts parted by financial pressure from the mother, Mrs. Holden, who brainwashed her daughter into marrying money instead," Jeremy informed him sardonically.

"I see. So Hawthorne wheedles his way in to Rutherford Hall under the pretext of helping Lord Rutherford compile his memoirs, while his real motive is to get back with the Lady in question. Unfortunately for him, Rutherford gets wise to their illicit affair...and seals his own death warrant," the inspector said, his eyes gazing out of the window, reflecting on this new theory.

"It's a possibility. After all, it would be decidedly convenient for them if they could get their hands on Rutherford's money and get him out of the way in one shot," Jeremy said simply.

"So Lady Celia stabs him, but he doesn't die, and Mr. Hawthorne finishes the half done job by strangling him!" the inspector said, with a growing conviction that this new theory was more plausible.

"And where would Miss Jones, the barmaid, come in?" Jeremy asked.

"Well, if they were having an illicit affair, they would have to arrange clandestine meetings, and Miss Jones probably saw them and threatened to tell all. This is a small village, and although she may not have known them in the social sense, she must have known who they were. But here's the interesting part that ties this up... We found about four thousand pounds in cash amongst Miss Cindy Jones' personal effects. And as you know, about the same amount of money went missing from the Rutherford Hall. She was carrying a suitcase full of clothes, and the money was found hidden in a pair of stockings. Looks as though she was planning to leave the village for good with the money she got by blackmailing them," the inspector surmised, feeling rather pleased with his deductive powers.

Jeremy had a doubt. "But why kill her if her plan was to leave the village for good anyway?"

"Because she would always be a threat. A witness to their affair who could tie them to Lord Rutherford's murder, and they couldn't afford not to silence her. Besides, everyone knows that blackmailers can never be trusted. They usually bleed their victims till their pockets are dry or till they are dead," was the inspector's reply.

"It's a theory alright. You did say that you had Mr. Hawthorne brought here for questioning?" Jeremy asked.

"Yes. We had, but owing to the fact that Sergeant Wilder went off the deep end and somewhat re-arranged his face, we will have to wait. The doctor is attending to him at the moment. I'm afraid Mr. Hawthorne may quite possibly be suffering from a broken jaw," the inspector told Jeremy.

"But why on earth would Sergeant Wilder...?" Jeremy asked, leaving his question hanging in the air.

"When Mr. Hawthorne came to the police station, he heard that the body of the young woman had been identified as the local barmaid. He made an unfortunate comment in front of the sergeant ...something on the lines of how he was right all along about a 'buxom wench' being involved in this affair," the Inspector made a face.

"And?"

"The sergeant was already upset, owing to the fact that Miss Jones had been a close friend of his at one time, and Mr. Hawthorne's unfortunate choice of words regarding the victim probably sent him right over the edge. I think its best that I take Wilder off this case," the inspector said wearily.

"I see," Jeremy said, digesting this new piece of information. And then, as an afterthought he added, "On the other hand, it may be a better idea to keep the good sergeant on the case. The fact that he is now emotionally invested in finding the murderer might just work wonders in your favour."

Chapter Seventeen

Burt Hopworth had been kept in the holding cell at the police station.

"Why have I been dragged here? I demand to see Sergeant Wilder. I demand an explanation!" he yelled at the middle aged guard who was busy making a meal of an overstuffed sandwich.

"You're in no position to make any demands, son. S'far as I know, you've been brought for questioning in a murder case," the guard replied, taking another bite of his sandwich.

"What? I have absolutely nothing to do with any blasted murder case. You have no right to keep me here without any charge. You had better release me soon, or I'll miss my ship to Africa damn it!" Burt said, banging at the bars in his frustration.

"I'll have no more cheek from you, lad. As far as I know, you can kiss your ship goodbye. I'm guessin' you're going to be here a while," the guard grinned sadistically, showing yellow, tobacco-stained teeth before letting out a loud satisfied burp to appreciate the large sandwich he had just eaten.

"Bloody bollocks! I know my rights. What's wrong with you coppers? Always blinkin' framing the wrong man for just about anything...just because you're too sodding lazy and too bloody dumb to crack a case. Just hauling me here because I have a past isn't going to save your arse you know. I'm going to every paper with my story of police harassment!" Burt shouted back.

The guard was beginning to enjoy himself and had thought of a rather juicy comeback about his rear end, but just then Sergeant Wilder strode into the holding cell area and said, "Oh, there you are Burt. I'm very sorry we had to detain you like this old boy. I was away working on this case and found out about your arrival just now. Guard, open up will you. C'mon move it...waiting for Christmas, are we?"

Grudgingly, the guard opened the lock on the cell door.

"Thank heavens you're here, Steven. What's all this about then?" Burt asked him as they headed up the stairs to the main hall.

"Murky case up at the hall. Old Rutherford's been stiffed. We're all clueless at this point, and unfortunate for you, that Betsy saw you up at the Hall that night, and that Holden woman found your note to your mum. I kept my mouth shut about your visit. Of course, I know you had nothing to do with it, but one thing led to another, and the inspector realised you were there the same evening someone chose to do the old man in. He still doesn't know that you stayed at my house through your visit and let's keep it that way. I don't want him taking me off the case because I withheld important information...That's how he'll see it. Anyhow, he insisted you be brought back for questioning. Tough luck, old boy. But I'm sure you'll make it through. It's just a matter of time before we find out who really killed him. But hey, now it's your turn. What's all this I hear about a Mrs. Burt Hopworth? Secret wedding? No invitation for your oldest friend, eh?" Steven chaffed him.

"Oh no. Left to me, you'd be my best man at a church wedding! You know how mum always wanted that. But Cindy wouldn't hear of it. She was absolutely insistent that we tell no one, including Mum, until we were safely ensconced in our new home in Africa. She said it was either that or nothing. She wouldn't take no for an answer. She seemed so unlike herself, almost as if she were ashamed of telling anyone we were going to be married. And with my prison record, I couldn't blame her. So, we were to get married quietly at the registrar's at Southampton before the sailing. I even got a special marriage license and everything. She made me promise that I wouldn't tell anyone about it, including you, mum and a long list of all the people we both knew here, so you see, I had to leave out the 'plans for marriage' bit when I told you about my plans for Africa," Burt told him, explaining the situation.

"Wait a minute, Burt. You are talking about Cindy... Cindy Jones?" Sergeant Wilder asked, with a puzzled look.

"Who else? Yes, I know you all thought it was over once I was sent to prison. But we had been engaged,

Steven, for so long...you know, practically since we were kids, and that kind of thing is hard to let go. Some months ago she showed up at my lodgings, if you can call that God awful place I was living in, that. She was really upset about it all and told me she wanted me to take her away from here. That all she wanted was to be married to me and get away from England. She was the one who put the idea of going to Africa in my head in the first place. She'd read in some paper or other about how white men and women were going to Africa for greener pastures and setting up their lives there. It had never occurred to me before. You know the rest...I sent out some feelers and then, like a miracle, this offer came. I'd never seen her happier. She was so excited about it all...starting a new life in a home of her own. She talked about having children. She wanted four!" Burt said with a faint smile.

Sergeant Wilder said with a sad smile, "Goodness. I can just picture the two of you with four African brats running about the place. I had no clue you two were still engaged. Why didn't she just trust me, or why didn't you, for that matter? Why didn't you both tell me? I could have helped you. It's all so sad. So what went wrong then?"

"She never turned up at our meeting point. She was supposed to meet me in the woods near the small bridge after I met mum, but she just wasn't there. So I took a chance and went to the pub thinking that she was getting her last minute goodbyes in, but they said they hadn't seen her either. It seems she had given her notice after closing the night before, and no one had seen her since. Then I went to her lodgings and Mrs. Potter told me she had packed a couple of hours ago and left. But she never showed up. It's like she did a disappearing act on me! She could have just told me that she changed her mind and that she didn't want to marry me after all, and that would've been the end of it! I would've sailed for Africa any which way. It's not like I had anything here in England to hang about for. Confounded women! Why can't they just be straight with a man?" he said angrily.

"Blimey! So you don't know? And had nothing to do with it?" Sergeant Wilder asked him incredulously.

"Know what? Do what? Talk straight man," Burt said impatiently.

"I think you had better sit down, Burt," Sergeant Wilder told him.

"Why do I have to sit down? Stop treating me like an old woman!" was Burt's response.

"Right. Thing is, Burt... Cindy was found strangled to death in the woods last evening," he told him straight out.

Burt let out a cry and sank into the chair behind him.

"It can't be. She can't be dead. There must be some mistake!"

"I'm afraid there's no mistake. She's dead, old man. Let me get you a glass of water," Sergeant Wilder said quietly.

"Bloody hell...when has a glass of water ever helped!" Burt said, his head in his hands.

"And it gets worse. Her time of death would coincide with about the time you said you were going to meet her in the woods...that is, if you were going to meet her right after your visit to the hall. I remember you telling me you were going up to the hall to pick up the money and say goodbye, around sevenish, if my memory serves me," Sergeant Wilder said.

"Yes, but I got delayed. Mum came late. And after that, when I went towards the study to say goodbye to Sir Charles, I saw his wife running out with blood on her. And then I heard the scream. I panicked and left for the woods. With my record, I didn't need any more trouble with the police. By the time I got to the woods to look for Cindy, it would've been at least eight. I thought she got tired of waiting for me – it was awfully cold that night, and I thought she went to the pub or something. She knew that would be the first place I'd look for her," Burt said, the news of Cindy's death slowly sinking in.

"Unlikely that she would lug her baggage all the way to the village in that weather. If I were in her shoes, I'd much rather have just waited there for you. Remember, it was an awful night. Think carefully man, did you see anyone else or any sign of her...or luggage...anything at all, while you were looking for her?" Sergeant Wilder asked.

"No. I didn't spot another soul till I got to the village... Couldn't see much at all in the woods either. There was such a fog that night. I had the flashlight on and just kept calling out for her from time to time, as I walked through the woods. When I got no response, I just started walking towards the village hoping she would be there. And all that time, you say, she was lying there, in the woods, strangled? Who would do such a thing?" Burt said, a haunted look in his eyes.

"Could've been a passing tramp, but I think we'd better get you a good lawyer all the same, Burt. You're going to need one," Sergeant Wilder said, grimly.

"You don't believe my story? You think I killed her?" he asked Sergeant Wilder, with a touch of surprise in his voice.

"I believe your story, old man, but you have to admit, to anyone else, it's going to sound a bit thin. Not only were you there in the vicinity when she was killed, but according to you, she was in the woods waiting to meet you when she was strangled, allegedly by someone else. *No one else knew she was going to be there, Burt!* And you've got no alibi. Now, I'm not saying it, but others are bound to draw different conclusions...seeing as no one else seems to have any reason to bump Cindy off like that," he concluded in a professional tone.

"Oh God! I'm going to hang, for something I didn't do, aren't I?" Burt said, sounding lost and defeated.

"Not if I have anything to do with it. If you didn't do it, and I believe you, I'm going to try my darndest to find out who did. You can rely on that," Sergeant Wilder said, with a determined look.

Chapter Eighteen

Around 9:30 in the morning, Jeremy drove to Rutherford Hall. As he brought his car to the front drive, Rachel ran down the steps. She had been awaiting his arrival.

"Good morning, beautiful! I missed you," he said conspiratorially in her ear as he gave her a chaste kiss on the cheek. He was being conservative. They were visible from all the front windows of the house. Rachel was glowing in a bright red sweater dress that was tight enough to show all her womanly curves.

"I dreamt about you all of last night. Can't wait to get my hands on you again," she said in his ears, a naughty smile lighting up her eyes.

"Whoa! Young lady. I'm an old man, remember..." Jeremy laughed out.

"Yes, practically a fossil by now. I'm going to visit your cottage at four in the afternoon today. Alone. You had better be there, Mr. Fossil," she informed him, with an unspoken promise in her eyes.

"I shall be delighted to welcome you home, my beauty," Jeremy smiled at her, thinking to himself, How did I get so lucky?

"Come along now. You have some explaining to do to Mums," she told him saucily.

"You told her about our..." Jeremy asked, blushing a deep red to match her sweater.

"About the case, silly! She wants to know what you've found out, so you can stop having a heart attack now. Must keep that ticker in shape for later," she said with a mischievous smile.

"Oh, ah yes...the case. Of course! I was with Inspector Parker last night after I left here," Jeremy said, relief flooding over him. He would have to deal with the complications this affair would cause later, but he was grateful not to have to do it now.

"Tsk, tsk. You're lucky I have no Othello-like qualities... leaving me alone here to spend the rest of the evening with Parker," she said, narrowing her eyes into slits.

"Yes. Quite. Can't blame you, given what scintillating company Parker is, and the police station being such a romantic place and all that," he deadpanned right back at her.

"Hmm. So what's his take on Ms. Cindy Jones' untimely departure, then?" she asked him seriously.

"Oh, so you already know who the victim was?" he asked.

"Yes. Did I mention it's a small village?"Rachel answered.

"Hmm. He thinks she was blackmailing Mr. Hawthorne and Lady Celia, and they decided to do her in," he told her.

"Now, that would have been interesting if it weren't such a hare-brained idea. Why on earth would he presume...?" Rachel asked in a puzzled tone.

"I may have had something to do with it. I told him the gist of the story Hawthorne spent an hour narrating to us the night of the murder, and the inspector decided the angle was ripe for investigation. And considering the missing money from the Hall was found in the girl's belongings, it may not be as hare-brained as it seems," Jeremy explained.

"Oh! I didn't know that! Now that is interesting!" Rachel said, looking thoughtful.

Then, after a pause, she added, "I think we'd better postpone our rendezvous to tomorrow Jeremy. I think I'm going to make some calls on people in the village this afternoon."

"You're going to nose about?"

"Yes."

"Would you like me to come along?"

"No. That would spoil it all."

"You remember what I told you about being careful. Keep in mind while you're poking about, that there is a murderer on the loose, and we don't want you on his or her radar."

"Yes of course. I shall be the soul of discretion itself."

"Why do I have trouble believing that?"

"Trust me. I can be quite discreet if I set my mind to it!"

"And you will report everything you learnt, to me?"

"Yes. I'll do that. Perhaps you can drop by for an early dinner and I'll fill you up with anything new I find about this Cindy girl."

"I may not be back in time for dinner. I've just had an idea that I ought to drive up to London and meet up with some old friends at the Yard. I have a theory about this case that I want to hash out with some old hands at the Yard."

"How exciting! What is it? Do tell me."

"All in good time, my beautiful. Once I get back."

"So when do you think you'll be back then?"

"By tomorrow afternoon. I'll be at the Yard and then stay the night at my club. Here are the numbers," he said, taking out a card and handing it over to her. "Ring me if you need me."

II

After breakfast with the family, Jeremy had left, and Rachel cornered the parlourmaid as she was clearing the breakfast things.

"Suzie?"

"Yes, Miss?"

"What do you know about the girl that was killed - Cindy Jones? Were you friends with her? Did you know her well?"

"Yes Miss...I mean, no Miss. I mean, we weren't real friendly like, but I knew all about her. Betsy used to tell me stories about her. A bad lot she was, attracting men all the time in that pub she worked at. Last we heard, she had got her claws into Sergeant Wilder, the poor sod, and now it looks like she got back to her old ways, mixed up again with a bad lot and ended up dead. I feel sorry for him. Still, seeing as it's not nice to speak ill about the dead, God rest her soul, but she did get mixed up with all sorts, that girl," Suzie said disapprovingly, taking a high moral ground.

"You mean she was attractive to men?" Rachel asked her with a faint smile.

Suzie blushed and said, "She was pretty, Miss, but in a wrong way. I thought she was common like, with all that red hair and them cheap, showy clothes. But Betsy knew her from the time they were girls. So she says. They were neighbours, Miss."

"What about Miss Jones' parents?"

"Oh, she hadn't got any, Miss."

"Eh? Oh, you mean they're dead?"

"Don't know Miss. All's I know is that she's always stayed with her aunt, Mrs. Potter, in the village."

"Do you think Betsy can take me to meet Mrs. Potter, Suzie?"

"If you don't mind my asking, why Miss?"

"Oh Suzie, I just want to pay my respects. However she may have been, a young girl like that cut down in her youth. It's all so sad." *Besides, I need to know who is killing all these people and get to the bottom of this,* Rachel thought to herself.

"Right, Miss. Very kind of you to think so, Miss. I'll ask Betsy, Miss. It's her afternoon off today. P'raps she can take you to meet Mrs. Potter today."

"Thank you, Suzie. You are a dear."

III

Betsy had grumbled to Suzie about having to accompany Rachel across to meet Mrs. Potter on her afternoon off.

"What? On my one afternoon off! I have plans, Suzie! Gracie and me were going to catch the matinee of Gilda again and get a nice tea later, and now you've gone and spoilt it all! And what do these people at the hall want to go interfering with Mrs. Potter for, anyhow? She has enough to do, what with the police and reporters crawlin' in and out of her house all day botherin' her, trying to find who killed Cindy an' all!" she complained to Suzie.

"Oh dear. I am sorry, Betsy. I didn't know. Miss Rachel said she wanted to pay her respects. She's feeling sad for her and all that, and I just thought it would be alright if I told her you'd take her over... I'm sure it won't take long. I am sorry. Really I am. I should've asked you before."

"Oh well. It's not your fault. I s'ppose I might as well get it over with. I don't think she'll spend a lot of time there anyhow. P'raps I can still get to the theatre in time for the matinee."

Chapter Nineteen

Dennis was brought into Inspector Parker's room by a constable after the doctor had ministered to his bruises.

"Take a seat, Mr. Hawthorne. I hope your jaw is better. I do apologize for the Sergeant's strong reaction to your comments," Inspector Parker said, not sounding apologetic in the least. It was evident that he did not condone either party's behaviour.

"I'm fine, now, but that Sergeant needs a straitjacket. How the hell was I to know she was his girl?" Dennis said in an angry tone.

"Let's not jump to conclusions. Sergeant Wilder was just an old friend of the victim," the inspector clarified, with a hint of a smile.

"Blimey! In that case, he's even more barmy than I gave him credit for," Dennis retorted.

"Now, the reason I've asked you to come in is to ask you if you are missing a Mother of Pearl cufflink, Mr. Hawthorne?"

"Yes, as a matter of fact I am. Why?"

"Right. Is this it?" the inspector asked casually.

"Yes. Thank you. Where did you find it?" Dennis replied, sounding faintly worried.

"Mr. Hawthorne, I am arresting you for the murders of Lord Charles Rutherford and Miss Cindy Jones. Anything you say may be..."

At this point, Dennis cut in. "What are you on about? I don't even know any Cindy Jones. And I certainly didn't kill Rutherford."

"Your cufflink was found in the priest's hole alongside Lord Rutherford's body. It must've fallen off in your effort to stash the body in the priest's hole," Inspector Parker said matter-of-factly.

"Okay. Alright. Look, I did put his body in the priest's hole but I didn't kill him or this woman, "Dennis said, his hands in front of him, a hunted look in his eyes.

"Right. Just one more question. How long had Miss Jones been blackmailing you and Lady Celia?"

"What? Blackmailing me and Celia for what?" Dennis asked, incredulity written all over his face.

"I know everything, Mr. Hawthorne, so it's best you come clean. You killed Lord Rutherford because he found out about the affair you were having with his wife. And then you strangled Miss Jones after paying her the blackmail money that you got Lady Celia to procure for you from the safe."

"Wait! You're making a terrible mistake. I did not kill him, I tell you. Or whoever this Jones woman was. There was no blackmail. There was no affair. I don't understand where or how you got the idea from. Yes, I am and have always been in love with Lady Celia, but if you think she's the type that would cheat on her husband, you couldn't be more wrong about her."

"So she doesn't cheat on her husband. She's not the type. But if her husband winds up dead, would she be the type to fall into her lover's arms for consolation, eh?" Inspector Parker asked, with a touch of sarcasm.

"You are impertinent Sir! How dare you!" Dennis shouted.

"Come now, you and the Lady can give all your explanations for the double murders at the trial, to interested parties," was the inspector's reply.

"Don't tell me you've arrested her as well?" Dennis asked, horror creeping into his voice.

"I will be, shortly," Inspector Parker replied.

"This is insane. You have no case. I'd like a lawyer," Dennis shouted.

II

It was close to one in the afternoon when Jeremy turned the car towards Piccadilly Circus. As he slowed for the traffic, he heard the newspaper boy in the corner shout out in a sing song voice, *"Double Murder! Read all about it. Famous Author Arrested..."*

There was a crowd of people buying the tabloid fresh off the noon press.

He stopped the car, leaned out of the window of the two-seater and whistled to the boy. The boy made a quick roll of the paper and, in a practiced throw, tossed it expertly towards Jeremy. He caught the paper with one hand and tossed a coin at the boy who, in turn, caught it adeptly.

Jeremy unrolled the tabloid. There was a large file picture of Dennis Hawthorne staring back through brooding eyes at him from the front page. *Well, I'll be damned! Parker has gone and arrested the boy already!* Jeremy thought to himself. And there was also a scattering of photographs around the main write up which took up the entire front page, including a flattering picture of the beautiful, demure Lady Celia alongside a weather-beaten, smiling face of Lord Rutherford in tails, probably taken from Tattler. There was also a grainy image of Cindy Jones smiling saucily in a tight, off-shoulder black dress with her ample cleavage visible - a cheap imitation of the dress made famous by Rita Hayworth in Gilda. The bold footnote beneath it read, *'Sexy barmaid found strangled in the woods. Police suspect a crime of passion.'*

Wonder where they got the 'crime of passion' bit from. Jeremy wondered if there was any truth in it, because the inspector had not mentioned a sex angle when he had told him about the woman's strangulation. Tabloids! This was not the first time in his experience that half-baked information found its way to the tabloids and was dished out like a meal to the public.

Jeremy drove to the club where he read the rest of the paper in the silence of the reading room.

The coroner's report claimed that severe bruising had been found on Miss Cindy Jones' neck and the forensic exam results had shown that she had been strangled to death. The Medical examiner also found some old bruises on her body that point to a history of violence. The report also mentioned that since the victim was not *virgo intacta*, there was a possibility that she had been the victim of forced intercourse a month or so prior to her death, based on the findings that some of the bruises were over a month old.

A reliable source from the police force said that Mr. Dennis Hawthorne had been brought in for questioning and had broken down and made a full confession of his heinous crimes to the police.

The reporter was also tipped off that this coup had been pulled off by Inspector Parker and his able team on the basis of finding a single cufflink that had belonged to the suspect, next to the hiding place of Lord Rutherford's body at Rutherford Hall.

"Full confession! Rubbish! He's barking up the wrong wood, forget the tree," Jeremy muttered to himself, as he put the paper down in disgust.

Chapter Twenty

Rachel Markham, accompanied by a rather sullen Betsy, was having tea with Mrs. Potter in the small sitting room of the cottage. The room was shabby yet cheerful, with a brown floral patterned wall paper, faded and peeling in places, very much like the owner herself, Rachel mused. Mrs. Potter had on a much used yet clean, printed frock and cardigan that was hanging fussily over a portly frame. Despite the sunlight coming in through the windows, the room seemed strangely dark. There seemed to be too many things all over the place, china dogs, frilly lamp shades, vases with dried flowers, picture frames covered in sea shells from a holiday somewhere, all coming together to make the futile attempt at gentility very noticeable. The creaking wicker chairs were stuffed with faded hand-embroidered cushions. *Must have taken her months, if not years, to embroider,* Rachel observed with a faint sense of amusement that testified to the notion that Mrs. Potter was definitely house-proud despite her straitened means of livelihood. It didn't take her long to notice that Mrs. Potter had given her tea in her best china cup set and made a fuss over the biscuits she had to make do with, given that she hadn't time to bake something for her. It touched her to be treated with so much reverence by someone she probably would not have recognised or even noticed on the main street.

"It's terrible all this. My 'earts broken, it is. Brought up the girl like my own. Now Miss, I'm not saying as that she was no trouble. But to get murdered 'orribly like that, a young 'un with her whole life ahead of her, it just breaks my 'eart," she said, sniffling. Her eyes were puffed up with shed tears.

"I do understand Mrs. Potter, and I am so very sorry for your loss. But I'm sure the police are doing all they can, and before long, they will find who did this," Rachel replied in a soothing voice.

"I know who did this. I told them it was that jailbird. Ever since he came out, he's been bothering my girl, he has. I want to see 'im hang," Mrs. Potter said indignantly.

"Surely you don't mean Mrs. Hopworth's son?" Betsy asked, her eyes as wide as saucers. Here was room for gossip that she could take back to the Hall.

"Who else? He's the devil, he is. And I told my Cindy to drop him after they hauled him off to jail, and she did. But as soon as he was out, he kept coming back and pestering her to get back with him. I even pushed her to go with that nice boy Sergeant Wilder instead. And she did go out with him a couple of times, but it was no good. My Cindy had nuthin' up there. She allus chose the wrong 'uns. And that's why, to my mind, she's wound up dead," Mrs. Potter said, with a deep conviction in her voice.

"Did she tell you anything about him ever hitting her? The police report says she had old bruises on her?" Rachel asked.

"I wouldn't know. She never told me anything. But I wouldn't put it past that devil. I did hear her have a flamin' row with him once, and after that, she went all quiet like."

"When was this?"Rachel was suddenly alert.

"About two months ago. She had been all quiet, and then one morning, she suddenly said she had to go out. She wouldn't tell me where. She was out the whole day, and I was beginning to worry. It got quite dark, and I heard voices out near the woods. I went out, and I could make out Cindy in the distance talking to him. They were shouting at each other. They were having a scuffle and I 'eard her screaming, 'Leave me alone you pig.' So I shouted out to her, 'Cindy, what's going on? Who is that?' That must've scared him off because, five minutes later, she came in looking all frightened, tired and washed out," Mrs. Potter said.

"And you are sure it was Burt Hopworth in the woods?" Rachel asked her.

"Well, it was dark but who else could it've been? I asked her when she came in if she'd been with that devil again and she said, 'Not now Auntie. I have to think.' And went to her room."

"This may sound odd, Mrs. Potter, but may I see her room? She may have inadvertently left some clues behind that may help the police catch whoever did this," Rachel asked hopefully.

"Sure, Miss, but the police have already been through everything, and Cindy had packed almost everything except for a few clothes and things she didn't like."

"Still. It's possible that the police may have missed something that would only strike another woman as odd. Please, it may help," Rachel said, trying to convince her.

"Well alright. I s'ppose it can do no harm," Mrs. Potter said hesitantly, not wanting to upset her distinguished guest from the hall.

They walked past the kitchen, through a narrow corridor to a door at the end. Mrs. Potter opened the painted cream door and held it open.

Rachel walked in, followed by her and Betsy, and asked Mrs. Potter hopefully, "Did Cindy leave behind any letters or a diary?" After all, in most mystery novels, including the one she was reading, the detective usually unravelled the mystery with diaries holding cryptic clues, or letters conveniently left behind, even half charred in fireplaces. All one had to do was read between the lines and voila!

"No, Miss. My Cindy was never one to read and write much. She could just about read, but she wasn't one to write much."

So much for life imitating art, thought Rachel as she began to observe. The room was in disarray, as if the occupant had left with very little notice, and yet all the information pointed to the fact that Cindy had planned this trip beforehand.

Why did she pack her things last minute? She gave her notice at the pub the night before. Why did she wait until the last minute to pack her luggage?

"Is that her picture?" Rachel asked Mrs. Potter as she got up to take a closer look at a frame on a side table still crammed with knick-knacks that Cindy had obviously not bothered to pack.

Rachel took a closer look at a picture of Cindy in an off-shoulder, tight fitting black dress posing in front of a painted cardboard car, the kind they have at fairs and carnivals for people to pose in front of. She looked happy, her smile was trusting and carefree. Like a girl who loved life. It was hard to believe that she was now a body with a toe tag on a cold stone slab in a mortuary. Rachel found her eyes filling up with tears and said, "She was very pretty." There was a catch in her throat.

Betsy had come up to look at the picture in Rachel's hand and exclaimed, "Why! This must be a new picture. The dress in the picture, why, that's the same dress we had made together just a few months ago. Cindy loved clothes, Miss. She spent all her money on buying material, cutting out pictures of frocks from fancy magazines and then stitching them 'erself. She was a good seamstress. This one is the copy of the Gilda dress. She bought two yards of silk for this!"

Mrs. Potter spoke through her sniffling, "Yes, and fat lot of good it did 'er. I kept tellin her not to waste all her money trying to look all actressy but she wouldn't listen. She wasn't a bad girl, Miss but she gave out that sort of look, a bit tart like, and that's what got 'er killed."

"Oh, come now, Mrs. Potter. I'd say she just had her own sense of style, and there's no use blaming the girl if she was pretty and liked to dress up. It only shows that she had spirit! I'd rather you blame the unhinged person who mercilessly killed a beautiful young girl in her prime," Rachel said, anger building up in her voice.

"There's that I s'ppose, Miss. But I can tell you, Miss, if she were more ordinary like, she would still be alive."

"But that's just it, Mrs. Potter – that's what makes me so angry. Just because a girl comes from a humble home doesn't mean she's not allowed to hope and dream. Cindy obviously had hopes of bettering herself, and to my mind, that's an admirable trait. Now then, let's try and find something, anything, that will help us get closer to the truth. Do you mind if I look in the wardrobe?"

"It makes no difference to me Miss. You can look anywhere. Nothing's going to bring 'er back 'ere Miss," Mrs. Potter said, as a fresh flood of weeping consumed her.

"There, there, Mrs. Potter, even if we can never bring her back, we owe her justice by helping the police catch whoever did this. Betsy, why don't you take Mrs. Potter out to the kitchen and make her a fresh pot of tea. I'll see what I can find here."

"Yes, Miss. Can I bring you a cup here, Miss?" Betsy asked Rachel, over her shoulder as she steered Mrs. Potter out of the room.

"No, thank you, Betsy. I won't be long."

After they left, Rachel walked towards the small cheap wooden wardrobe standing in the corner and opened the door. To her surprise, she saw it was still half-filled with clothes neatly stacked. *She did love her clothes. Only someone who cares about clothes would leave them behind this tidily.* There was no space to hang anything, but everything was folded neatly. There was no disarray here. There were neat piles of faded old jumpers on one shelf and two or three skirts in another. The second shelf contained some old nightdresses, and even two old dresses that were clearly out of fashion now and hence left behind. Rachel bent down and saw a few pairs of well-worn tattered shoes on the lowest shelf. One pair that had a cheap silver buckle wrenched out, sat neatlyononeside,asiftheownerdidn'thavethehearttothrow them out and yet hadn't bothered to get them fixed either. On the shelf above that, there was a much-used faded grey bathrobe. Just next to that she saw a crumpled up swathe of black cloth. It looked like silk. Rachel pulled it out. It was the black dress from the picture. It had a tear down the side as if it had got caught on a nail. She folded it and put it back.

She looked about the room at the chest of drawers. There's got to be something here. Rachel walked towards the chest and opened the first drawer, which had some broken pieces of cheap imitation jewellery, satin ribbons, fancy buttons and haberdashery odds and ends. The second one had old stockings and underwear. The last drawer had magazine cut-outs of fashionable women in beautiful clothes and jewellery. There were also some papers. Rachel unfolded them and saw that they were bills for different items, various pieces of material and clothing items, a pair of shoes and the latest one dated a week ago was for a travel bag from the village general store.

Rachel put everything back and sighed. She had found nothing.

Chapter Twenty One

Jeremy had driven back from London as soon as possible and headed straight to the police station. Something told him that his intervention was required now. Inspector Parker had already arrested Dennis Hawthorne and was probably in a hurry to arrest Lady Celia next. He got to the police station just in time. Inspector Parker was about to leave for Rutherford Hall. Jeremy was sure that they needed more concrete evidence against the couple in question. Besides, it seemed far too convenient to assume that, together, they had contrived to kill Rutherford and then kill Cindy Jones. After all, the police had no real evidence to go on except for the cufflink being found in the priest's hole. That may well have been planted there by someone else to incriminate Dennis Hawthorne. They needed more time and more evidence.

Years of experience told him that something was wrong with the scenario, and he wanted to prevent the police from making another wrong arrest. He spent ten minutes with Inspector Parker trying to explain his theory. By the end of it, he had managed to convince Inspector Parker not to arrest Lady Celia just yet. Instead, he suggested that they could get much closer to the truth if they interviewed her at Rutherford Hall.

They had driven together to the hall and asked for Lady Celia. Hopworth had shown them to the study, where she was going through the manuscript of her late husband's memoirs. The fire had been lit and the room looked cosy. She was dressed in a simple black wool dress, and yet the black wool against her alabaster skin had a stunning effect. *Mourning suits her,* was the thought that ran through Inspector Parker's mind.

She greeted them in a business-like manner and then spoke to the inspector directly. "I know you've arrested Dennis, but I simply can't get myself to believe that Dennis could have hated Charles enough to kill him with such violence!" Celia said with a shudder, as if someone had walked over her grave.

"Lady Celia, we'd like to ask you a few questions, pertaining to this case, if that's alright?" the inspector asked in an equally business-like tone.

"Certainly, Inspector. If you'll excuse me, I suddenly feel cold. I'll just get a wrap from my room and meet you back here in a moment."

Ten minutes later, Celia joined Jeremy and the inspector in the study. She had donned an exotic Indian black cashmere shawl, hand embroidered with delicate gold thread, over her dress.

The inspector and Jeremy were already seated in armchairs near the study table, as she re-entered the room. Jeremy had gotten up to pull an armchair closer to the fireplace for Celia.

She smiled and thanked him before making herself comfortable. Something told her that this was going to be a long interview. It felt strange to her that life had resumed so quickly and casually in the very room that had just witnessed passionate human emotions and a vicious murder. They say walls pick up emotional vibrations...that a house resonates with the frequency of events that take place in its rooms. She wondered if it were true, and if Charles was a disembodied entity, suspended somewhere, invisible to them, watching as they ate, spoke, lived and carried on with their lives as if nothing had transpired. It made her shudder.

The inspector's voice brought her back from her reverie. "Lady Celia, I needed to ask you a few questions regarding your relationship with your husband," Inspector Parker said in an even tone.

"Yes. I thought you might," was Celia's calculated reply.

"Lady Celia, if you don't consider it offensive, could you begin with how you came to be married to Lord Rutherford...there seems to be a rather large disparity in your ages," he said, coming right down to the brass tacks.

"Yes. It's funny that you think your question would offend me, Inspector. When we first got married, even the marriage registrar at London seemed quite curious. I'm sure if people weren't restrained by social etiquette and politeness, I would have been asked that question a hundred times. Even when people from the village came over to call on me, as they would on any new bride in the vicinity, I could read their minds. The younger women wanted to ask me, 'What's it like being married to a man thirty years older?' and the older women gave off that, 'I'm sure she married him for his money!' expression. I can tell you, Inspector, I would have been far more comfortable if they had done just that - asked me straight, why I married him or why he married me, instead of jumping to their own preconceived conclusions. But as they say, it's not fair to expect everyone to understand your journey, especially if they've never had to walk your path."

"That's quite a deep statement coming from someone so young, Lady Celia," Jeremy observed.

"Perhaps, because my mental age does not correspond with my chronological age Mr. Richards. If I were to tell you, that some people go through a great deal of life, in the shortest possible time, would you believe it?"

"Yes. I would. From what I've heard, I do believe that your singular childhood in India and the events that followed have embellished you with experiences that go beyond what most people ordinarily experience over a lifetime. If I'm not wrong, yours, Lady Celia, has been an extraordinary life of extremes. Starting with *extreme isolation* growing up as a lonely child on a secluded tea plantation with a friend who visited only through his summer vacations, *extreme grief* when your only constant companion, your dog died, *extreme despair* to lose the only parent who understood and supported you and then the final experience of sudden and *extreme poverty* after his passing." And he thought to himself, *add extreme beauty to that lethal combination and there was a dangerous possibility of extreme consequences – good or bad, for any man who got involved with her.* Hers was an extreme beauty, capable of eliciting extreme emotions from otherwise sane and sensible men.

"Detective, everything you said is true. You seem to have done your homework quite thoroughly. Scotland Yard must have been very sorry to lose someone as sharp as you," she said, looking at him directly.

"Ah! There you are mistaken Lady Celia, for I can tell you quite honestly, that is not the case, and that several people must have heaved a common sigh of relief to see me go," was Jeremy's sardonic, yet honest reply.

She smiled and said, "I can believe that, Detective. Formidable intelligence, such as yours, often has that impact and can make people rather uncomfortable. However, getting back to your question Inspector, after a life of such extremes, as Detective Richards has been kind enough to point out, it was such a relief for me to find that someone as understanding and well, *ordinary*, as Charles, *wanted* to marry me. I would be dishonest if I said his wealth was the only thing that attracted me to him. Although, to be honest, the fact that he was also wealthy give me a certain sense of security for my future. I'm sure you must've read Cinderella as a child, Inspector. The fact that my Prince Charming happened to be thirty years older than me, didn't, in any way, take away from the fact that he rescued me from a grim, cheerless and uncertain future that most young gentlewomen with meagre means like mine, have to look forward to."

"Thank you, Lady Celia, for being so forthright. That was most informative. I have another equally blunt question I'd like to ask you."

"Fire away, Inspector," Celia responded.

"What role did you have in Dennis Hawthorne's invitation to stay at Rutherford Hall?"

"What makes you think I had any role in that?" she asked with faint amusement.

"Well, I just assumed..." he faltered uncharacteristically.

"Don't, Inspector. Please, I beseech you to not assume or presume anything when it comes to me. Ask me, and I promise to give you a straight answer. And I can tell you with complete surety, that I did not have any hand in Charles' decision to invite Dennis to write his memoirs," She told him, her eyes holding his with an unflinching gaze and continued, "In fact, I was completely against it."

"This may sound like a stupid question to you, Lady Celia, but why were you against inviting Mr. Hawthorne here?" Inspector asked her cautiously.

"Inspector, do you believe in women's intuition?" Lady Celia asked him. When he grimaced and shook his head apologetically, she continued, "Yes, just as I thought. But I must ask you to believe that I had a premonition that his coming here would bring a great deal of unhappiness... and in some way put us in danger...and I was right. It did."

"Did you share this premonition with your husband, Lady Celia?" Jeremy asked her, in his quiet way.

"I did, but sadly, my husband was a man of the world and refused to believe me when I told him about the dream, or rather nightmare I had, about Dennis coming to this house. He brushed it off as indigestion and an over-active imagination, which he thought, was a result of my youthful fancies. Sometimes he was like that. At times he treated me as a fanciful child, but only when it suited him."

"I see. Was your married life normal? I mean with the age difference...and him treating you as a child?" Inspector Parker asked tentatively, hoping a question of such a personal nature would not shock and offend the young lady.

She looked at him for a moment, as if she was trying to suss out the motive behind the question, and then replied, "Yes Inspector. My husband may have been older and may have treated me like a child from time to time, but he was a perfectly fit and healthy man and was quite passionate when it came to our marriage bed, if that's what you are asking," she said, holding his gaze.

It was the inspector's turn to blush. She had turned the tables neatly and put him in a spot. "Er...ah... of course. I'm sorry I had to ask that, you see..." he said, fumbling to find words.

Although Jeremy was fighting to keep a straight face watching the inspector's discomfiture at having received a direct answer to a very personal question, he came to his rescue and broke the awkward silence that ensued.

He turned to Lady Celia, "Was there any particular reason for your husband to zero in on Mr. Hawthorne, to write his memoirs?" Jeremy asked, changing the subject.

"Yes. He had read his book and admired his writing style. He said Dennis had a way with words that could only be a God given gift. He had been searching for someone to put his memoirs to paper, and one day, when we were all at breakfast, Charles was reading out an article on upcoming young authors, when my mother could not resist boasting about us having known Dennis since he was a schoolboy. Charles got excited and asked her to get in touch with him. And that is how it all started."

"So your husband did not know about your past with Mr. Hawthorne?" Inspector Parker ventured cautiously.

"I had no 'past' with Mr. Hawthorne, Inspector. What Dennis and I had was an innocent friendship. I loved him, but not in the way you are insinuating. We were just childhood friends. I had no reason to tell Charles otherwise."

"I was given to believe that he proposed marriage to you, prior to your nuptials with Lord Rutherford?" Jeremy asked.

"That was just a boyish outburst, to my mind. We had met after ages, and he was just a boy back then. As you must know by now he is the imaginative and artistic type; I honestly think he confused our friendship with love. I had to turn him down. As I told you before, I did love him back then, but as one would love a dear friend and nothing more," was her reply.

Jeremy found himself thinking again, 'extreme beauty' had the ability to create that effect. Dennis obviously loved her with an extreme passion that was not reciprocated. A passion that she was not even aware of. Or was she? A passion that her woman's intuition had conveniently overlooked. *Or had it?*

Chapter Twenty Two

Three days later, Rachel and Jeremy were taking their usual post lunch walk through the cedar-lined walkways of Rutherford Hall. In the past few days, it had become a pleasurable habit for them to spend most of their afternoons together, talking about the case or taking walks together when the weather permitted. They walked until the house was out of view. Then they stopped to embrace and kiss each other. What had started in the summerhouse had now become a part of their daily routine. As the days went by, their passion for each other strengthened into a deep and passionate friendship. They looked forward to these times when they could be on their own, immersed in one another's company.

They resumed walking. It was surprisingly pleasant weather for the end of November and the afternoon sun covered the acres of rolling park land around them with a soothing golden glow. Rachel was in a beige sheath dress with a matching beige coat thrown over her shoulders. Jeremy took off his brown tweed jacket and carried it in the crook of his arm. He looked boyish in his thick brown cotton shirt and tweed trousers. Anyone observing them would have agreed that they made quite a handsome pair.

Rachel spoke, "You know, no matter what they say, I simply cannot get myself to believe that Dennis is responsible for killing Uncle Charles."

"I agree. But there is the matter of his cufflink in the priest's hole. What is your take on that?" Jeremy asked, curious to pick her brains.

"I have this strange idea that he may have moved Uncle Charles' body. You remember, that night, he simply flew off the handle because he thought Mum and Lydia suspected Celia had killed Uncle Charles?"

"Yes. I was there, remember?"

"What if Dennis had the same suspicion? He's so blindly in love with her that he would probably protect her till death, even if he knew she was capable of murder."

"That's very interesting. Come to think of it, he even mentioned something about her having a core of steel under that fragile facade. Do go on..."

"So I think, and knowing fully well that he is somewhat unhinged...to a great extent in fact, when it comes to Celia, he did for a while believe that she had in fact stabbed her husband to death. And all he did on finding Uncle Charles lying there, stabbed to death, was to simply move the body so he could get rid of it later and no suspicion would fall on Celia. He's the type of lover who wouldn't mind sacrificing his own life to ensure her safety."

"Really! And how would you know that about him? People say things that they hardly follow through when push comes to shove, you know!"

"Oh Jeremy, read his book! In it, the hero gives up his own life to save the woman he loves, forty years after she's dropped him like a hot potato for some rich Count Mondeco or some such idiot."

"Right. But Celia couldn't have murdered Charles because he was, in fact, strangled to death..." Jeremy said, the lights going on.

"Exactly darling! None of us knew that night that Uncle Charles had, in fact, been strangled to death. And to my mind, if Dennis hid his body because he thought Celia stabbed him, that proves his innocence beyond a doubt because how can a murderer possibly not know how the victim was killed!"

"But here's a thought for you. What if Dennis did strangle him and then shoved his body in the priest's hole?"

"No. He's simply not the type. I can't imagine Dennis with his fragile artistic temperament looking someone in the eye and strangling them to death. If I were to imagine him committing murder, I'd see him pushing someone off a precipice or using arsenic, for that matter. But strangling? Not a chance."

"There's some truth in that. If I had to do his psychological profiling, I'd probably come to the same conclusion."

"Besides, I don't think he even knew who Cindy Jones was, and I think that 'quelling the blackmailer' motive is simply bunkum."

The walk through the cedar-lined path was beautiful. Jeremy had gone silent, almost as if he were lost in his own world of thought. Rachel too was soaking in the beauty all around her. It was days like this that made her feel grateful for having taken birth in one of the most beautiful places on God's green earth. Her mind went back to that fateful night, and she thought of Dennis Hawthorne's description about the blazing colours of India, and decided that while she would have enjoyed a short holiday anywhere in the tropics, she was glad she lived in England with its peaceful muted colours. Even the rainy greys appealed to her delicate sense of beauty. And on days like this, when a simple walk across the grounds made one feel as if one was suspended in a world of honeyed gold, she felt truly blessed to be alive.

Jeremy's voice broke her reverie, "You seem awfully quiet suddenly. Something else on your mind?"

"Not really...just grateful to be here and alive, with you by my side. It's all so beautiful and peaceful," she answered with a smile.

"You are a peaceful girl," Jeremy observed, and took her hand in his. "Rachel, I think I'm in danger. I might just be falling in love with you."

"There's no danger in that. I like the idea. I like you. And I like this," she said with a smile, squeezing his hand tighter to drive home her words.

"I like it too. And the fact that we can spend so much time talking and the same amount of time in companionable silence if we want to, without finding it awkward."

They smiled at each other in perfect understanding.

"But we really should talk," he said.

"About what?" Rachel was curious.

"About you being half my age."

"Oh that! I told you before, Jeremy. I really do believe that age is just a number."

"You may not feel the difference today, my darling, but once you reach my age, your youthful folly in choosing me might hit you hard, because by that time, I'll be sixty and quite possibly a very cantankerous old man."

"Big difference. You're a cantankerous old man right now!" she laughed, her eyes shining with mischief.

"Is that so? In that case, let's go to my place right now and let me show you exactly how cantankerous I can get," he said in a mock threatening tone.

Rachel laughed even harder, "Only if you can catch me, old man," she said, as she broke into a sprint with him in hot pursuit.

It didn't take him long to catch her and kiss her again.

She squealed through her laughter, "By the time you get to sixty, Jeremy Richards, you'll probably be feebler than me, and I'll beat you off with a stick. So if anyone has to worry about youthful follies, it had better be you."

Chapter Twenty Three

The next day, Jeremy and Inspector Parker paid Dennis Hawthorne a visit in the holding cell.

"Detective Richards, this is madness. You can't possibly believe that Celia and I killed her husband and then that woman. The inspector has gone mad. He's got nothing but a cufflink to go on," Dennis said, shaking his head.

"I'm sure one can plead reasonable doubt, but Mr. Hawthorne, can I ask you a question?" Jeremy asked.

"Sure. If it's reasonable."

"Why did you put Lord Rutherford's body in the priest's hole?"

"Look, that's all I did. I promise. I did not kill him. I already told him that," Dennis said, pointing in the inspector's direction.

"But if you say you didn't, you are obviously trying to cover up for someone who did," the inspector stated.

"I'm afraid I'd rather let you lot hang me than tell you anymore. You can hang me if you like, but it'll be on your head that you sent an innocent man to the gallows," was Dennis' response.

"Hardly innocent, I'd say. Even if it's true that you did not kill him, you are withholding facts, obstructing the course of justice and are a bonafide accessory after the act then," Inspector Parker told him calmly.

Dennis stayed mum.

Jeremy spoke, "And if you are under some delusion that you are trying to protect a fair maiden from the gallows, you are even more dim-witted than I gave you credit for."

"And what is that supposed to mean?" Dennis asked angrily.

"Lord Rutherford was strangled to death by a man. So unless you think your fair maiden strangled him to death with her bare hands, you had better come clean," was Jeremy's response.

"But he was stabbed...I saw it with my own eyes!" Dennis blurted out.

"You saw him being stabbed?" Jeremy asked.

"Well, no. Not quite. You see, I was returning from the summerhouse. Mrs. Lydia Holden had sent me to investigate the note she had found from this Burt fellow."

"Yes, and?" Jeremy prodded him.

"And I didn't see anyone at the summerhouse, so I came back towards the study. Only when I got close to the French windows, I saw...er...something," Dennis said, his voice trailing off at the end.

"I'll tell you what you think you saw. You saw a certain lady pulling out a knife from a body and subsequently walk towards the French windows. And then, as she came out through the windows, you saw the blood on her and just assumed that she had committed murder. Hypothetically of course," Jeremy told him.

"Well yes...er...that just about fits...hypothetically, of course," Dennis agreed.

"Yes. And that fits with her story as well, about seeing someone come towards the study windows partially covered by the fog. She obviously did not recognize you," Jeremy informed him.

"Must've been the coat I was wearing at the time. I pulled it off the coat stand in the study before heading off for the summerhouse," Dennis explained.

"Then, in the madness of the moment, based on your presumption that the Lady had got fed up and killed her husband so she could be with you finally, you decided to shift the body so you could dispose of it later, somewhere far off, and save her from the gallows. Rather a stupid move for an intelligent man to make, wouldn't you say?" Jeremy asked, with one raised eyebrow.

"It didn't seem all that stupid at the time. I was confused. All I could think of, was that I had to cover up her link to the crime somehow, and old Rutherford had shown me the priest's hole a couple of days ago. It just seemed so easy. Without a body, the police would have one hell of a time proving that any crime had been committed. It would just have remained a missing person's case. And I would've been able to pull it off, if it hadn't been for Rachel's damned interference and her memory of the priest's hole. Dashed bad luck."

"Yes, and to top it, you managed to scare Celia senseless. You see, she thought you were the killer and that you were coming back to get her aswell. In her blind panic to get away from you, she nearly got herself killed. Not the smartest Romeo move you could've made for your Juliet, I'd say," Jeremy concluded.

II

Meanwhile, Sergeant Harolds was conducting the interrogation with Burt Hopworth. A steno was present in the room, taking notes. Burt had refused the offer of a lawyer to be present during interrogation.

He was not standing up well under police interrogation. He fumbled when he was asked about the nature of his relationship with Cindy Jones.

"I, well, I loved her. I mean, we loved each other. Since we were about seventeen. In the middle, we had parted ways because ahem...she didn't want to."

"I see. She didn't want to see you anymore. Why was that?"

"There would have been a technical difficulty in meeting frequently, owing to the fact that I was detained by her Majesty's government for a while. But over the past six months, we got back together."

"In what sense did you get back together?"

"Obviously not in the biblical sense! What sense do you think, Sergeant? We were going to be married."

"And yet, according to your own statement, she didn't show up to marry you."

"Because she was dead, you idiot! Somebody killed her!"

"Watch your tone, Hopworth. We are beginning to think that somebody might be you because she finally came to her senses and said she didn't want to marry you."

"That's rubbish. She came to me in London and asked me to marry her."

"So you say and we only have your word for it. Can you produce any witnesses?"

"Obviously not. She came to my rooms in the bachelor quarter. I was hardly going to invite my housemates to witness a private conversation with my girl."

"Was there anything in writing? A letter, perhaps, to prove that Miss Jones asked you to marry her?"

"Course not! I just told you it was a private conversation in my room. It was v-e-r-b-a-l, do you understand? And we did not have a steno taking notes through it."

"Do you have any letters to prove that Miss Jones was even remotely interested in you or your advances?"

"Unfortunately not. Cindy was never much of a letter writer."

"I see. According to Mrs. Potter's statement, you stalked her niece, harassed her and gave her no peace until she yielded to your unwelcome advances. Is that true?"

"Of course it's not true! Mrs. Potter must be potty! Besides, she hates me."

"With good reason perhaps, if you forced yourself time and again on this defenceless young girl."

"I think this interview is over."

"I'll tell you when it's over. Did you have a row with her, about two months ago, near her home?"

"No."

"Did you ever hit her?"

"No."

"Where were you on the night of 15th November, 1946; did you go into the woods bordering Rutherford Hall?"

"Yes. I was supposed to meet her there."

"At what time?"

"About 7:30ish. But I got delayed because my mother was late for our meeting on the grounds of the hall."

"Did you meet her?"

"Yes."

"You met Miss Cindy Jones? And what time was that?"

"No, I did not meet Miss Jones."

"But you just said you did."

"I thought you were asking about my mother, for God sakes! I met my mother. I did not meet Miss Jones."

"Where were you supposed to meet her? Miss Jones, that is."

"In the woods near a small bridge over the stream that separates Rutherford Hall from the woods."

"Did anyone else know you were supposed to meet her there?"

"Not to my knowledge. No."

"So you were the only one who knew she would be there at that time."

"Well, I suppose you could say that. But I wouldn't know if she told anybody else."

"Is it likely she told somebody else about meeting you there? Another friend or a girlfriend?"

"I can't be sure, but I know she was very secretive about our plan to marry. So no, I don't think it's likely."

"Why would she be secretive about her plans to marry you?"

"I've always assumed she was ashamed to tell anyone that she was marrying me, on account of my having done time in prison."

"Right. One last question. Did you strangle her to death?"

"No. I bloody well did not."

Chapter Twenty Four

The funeral had been kept low key owing to the publicity the case had generated. The church ceremony had also been kept simple and short. The police had managed to cordon off the cemetery as the bodies were sent to their final resting place. The church and the cemetery were on slightly higher ground, and as Lord Rutherford was lowered into the ground, Celia found the tears that she had held back over the past few days, flowed, and she allowed them to. It gave her some degree of peace as she realised that her husband's grave was on a windswept hill, very much like the hills depicted in the Albert Bierstadt paintings he had collected and loved so much. And she realised that she was going to miss him. His calm presence. The way he took care of everything, effortlessly, and with a natural grace. And then it hit her. She *had truly loved him.* She had loved the quality of gentleness he possessed. He had radiated a genuine love and goodness towards life and everyone around him, a rare and precious quality, to her mind. A quality that mirrored the memory, she carried in her heart, of her father Augustus Holden.

II

The next day, Lady Celia sat quietly in the visitor's chair facing Inspector Parker at the police station. Lady Elizabeth, Lydia Holden and Major Markham were seated in chairs next to her. Rachel was standing, leaning against the wall. Jeremy was by her side. Celia looked pale, and her eyes had a puzzled look in them. It had been hard for her to accept the fact that Dennis was still under suspicion for the murders.

Inspector Parker addressed her, "as you know, there have been certain developments in the investigation, and owing to some incriminating evidence having been found, we had earlier on arrested Dennis Hawthorne."

Celia spoke up, "Yes, but I still don't understand what connection Dennis had with my husband's death, Inspector."

Inspector Parker clarified. "Lady Celia, both you and Mr. Hawthorne were under suspicion till we cleared up some of the fog surrounding this case. We've now held Burt Hopworth on suspicion. There is still the matter of the stolen money found amongst Miss Jones' belongings that baffles us, and we need to find out how the money wound up with her if Burt Hopworth had indeed carried out the crimes on his own. We now know that he and Miss Jones were engaged to be married. We also have information from Mrs. Potter that he had a history of violence with the murdered girl. And, of course, it's public knowledge that he has done time for theft. We are still unclear as to what happened or the exact sequence of events that took place on the night in question. But at least we know now, that Mr. Hawthorne did not murder your husband. He just moved your husband's body after the murder was committed..."

Celia cut in, "But why? What would make Dennis do something like that?"

Inspector cleared his throat and said, "To our minds, it was a case of misplaced chivalry for you, Lady Celia."

"But that would mean that he thought I had...that I... No, he couldn't have," she faltered and then, regaining her composure after a pause, continued, "He knew I was very fond of my husband. Inspector, not many people know this, but I've always looked upon Charles as my saviour, and I was very grateful to him for all the kindness, generosity and love he showered me with. Dennis knew that...and he must've known that I loved Charles very much," Celia said with genuine emotion.

Inspector Parker spoke gently. "In my experience, human nature, as opposed to what most people claim, is really quite predictable. Mr. Hawthorne, by his own admission, made it perfectly clear that he was and still is, in love with you. And people in love often believe what they wish to believe. Rose tinted glasses and all that. Besides, the age difference between you and your husband probably strengthened his misguided notion that you were in an unhappy marriage. Perhaps, like many others, he couldn't quite bring himself to believe that you were truly in love with your husband, Lady Celia."

Celia spoke up, "And he would have been right. It's true. I never claimed that I was in love with my husband, Inspector. I loved him, yes, and I was fond of him and very grateful to be his wife, but I cannot honestly claim that I was in love with him."

"What's the bally difference? I simply don't get it," Major Markham said, looking baffled.

Rachel spoke up in Celia's defence, "Most men wouldn't, Daddy dear. I think what Celia is trying to say, is that loving someone is really quite a different kettle of fish than falling head over heels in love with someone. The former is a choice-based emotion, while the latter - well, let's just say that one has little or no control over the latter," she said, throwing a quick knowing glance in Jeremy's direction.

Lady Elizabeth gave her daughter a searching look and said, "Why, my dear, you suddenly seem to know a lot about love." Rachel blushed, but before she could respond, Major Markham spoke up.

"Poppycock! Girls and their idiotic notions! If you love someone, you love them. You don't go about murdering them!" he said in an irritated voice.

"On the contrary, Major, a number of murders are instigated exactly by that. What people call love... or volatile emotions parading under the guise of love. In legal parlance, we call them crimes of passion," Jeremy said with a sardonic smile.

Lydia Holden interrupted the direction the conversation was taking by saying, "Yes, but since you don't think Dennis murdered Charles, irrespective of whether or not he was in love with my daughter, what's that got to do with this case? Where are we in this case? I'd like to know who killed my son-in-law."

"That's exactly what we'd all like to know, Mrs. Holden," Inspector Parker said wearily and continued, "To that end, I'd like to ask you all to give your formal statements that will go on record for the inquest to be held this coming Monday."

"May I see Dennis? Is he still here?" Celia asked the inspector tentatively.

Lydia Holden spoke in a disapproving voice, "What do you want to see him for? He's got you into enough trouble as it is!"

Elizabeth also turned to Celia and said quietly, "I'm not sure that's a very wise idea, especially now, my dear."

"I agree," Major Markham said in bluff agreement with his wife. "Besides, I'd listen to her if I were you. The old girl is usually right about most things."

Celia spoke up in her own quiet way, "With all due respect James, I distinctly seem to remember, some years ago, neither you nor Elizabeth thought it was a very wise idea for Charles to marry me."

Lady Elizabeth intervened at this point, "Oh, but my dear, that was for very different reasons," she said, and by way of explanation to the inspector, she added, "It's true, you know, Inspector. I've always felt that men get irrational at a certain age, and I was quite opposed to this marriage in the beginning. We felt Charles was, well, besotted for all the wrong reasons. After all, it was only natural for us to be concerned about the age difference, more than anything else."

And the inspector found himself thinking that, 'anything else' could also translate to - being in a financially tight spot, they had probably been more worried about their share of the inheritance being further diminished by the brother taking what they had assumed Celia to be - a young fortune huntress, for a wife.

Rachel interjected, "Mother, please! How does age matter, if one can see how good two people can be for each other? Really, sometimes you can be so archaic..."

"Rachel, dear, don't argue with me unnecessarily. I don't know what's got into you lately. Besides, we all seem to be overlooking the fact that this is not the right time and place for a family squabble," Elizabeth said with finality, putting an end to the topic as Rachel rolled her eyes in defiance.

Despite the disapprovals voiced by the rest of her family, Celia spoke softly with renewed determination, "Inspector, I hope it's not too much of a bother, but I would like to see Dennis if you don't mind."

Inspector Parker responded to Celia, "That's alright, Lady Celia. We are about to release Mr. Hawthorne shortly. I'll take you to him once the statements are recorded."

Chapter Twenty Five

It had been a long day for everyone. The police had recorded the statements to be submitted at the inquest. Based on the joint statements given by Mrs. Holden and Lady Celia, Dennis Hawthorne had been released and was back at Rutherford Hall. It had come to light that Lydia Holden had indeed seen him head out towards the summerhouse, and by the time he had returned, which was duly inferred through Lady Celia's statement, Lord Rutherford had already been killed. Circumstantial evidence and his own confession pointed to his having hidden the body, but the overall consensus based on timelines, had been that he could not have committed the actual crime.

The news of Dennis Hawthorne's release and Burt Hopworth's arrest had spread like wildfire. Reporters had managed to swarm in on the grounds of Rutherford Hall, much to everyone's consternation. Luckily for them, it had started raining heavily and that had dispersed most of the sensation hunters. The French windows had been locked and the drapes had been drawn. Rutherford Hall had transformed into an able fortress that shielded its inmates from prying eyes and unwelcome visitors. They had all consumed a light supper and most of the family had retired early.

Jeremy had joined them for supper, and after supper, he and Rachel had moved to the privacy of the library for a postprandial nightcap. Jeremy told her about the statement Burt had given the police.

Jeremy spoke, "Somehow, darling, after going through everything, I'm getting the strange feeling that it wasn't Burt Hopworth either. I don't know why. Of course, he's obviously the most likely suspect with motives to boot, but *there's something that doesn't fit.* I mean, even if he did kill Charles, steal the money, then go and strangle his fiancé, *why was the money found in the dead girl's belongings and not on him?*"

"Oh, Jeremy, I don't know, but then who else could it be? We've eliminated Dennis, and now, if eliminate Burt from the list of suspects, there's hardly anyone left... well, apart from my father that is, and he had no reason to strangle the Jones girl. At least, I'm hoping he didn't..." Rachel said, shaking her head against the possibility.

"No, my dear. I doubt very much that your father went around strangling people that night," Jeremy said with a smile.

"Then there are no able bodied men left! Who could it possibly have been?" Rachel asked, wondering out loud.

Jeremy shook his head. He had no answer.

"That just leaves you, my darling. Did you strangle everyone?" Rachel asked him, as she leaned in for a kiss.

"No, it's just too much trouble and effort going about strangling people. I'm old and lazy now, remember? Even pushing people off precipices seems like a lot of hard work to me. Like Dennis' option two, I'd much rather slip arsenic into my victim's drink or something," he said and kissed her back.

"For me, it's even easier. All I have to do is make a home-cooked meal with my own hands, and people will just drop dead in agony."

"That good, huh?"

"The best. I'd advise you to stay in my good books so that I'm never tempted to cook for you."

"Thank you so much for the prior intimation, darling. I'll try to be on my best behaviour around you from now on. But now, I simply must bolt. Not on account of your threat to cook for me, but because these country roads are treacherous in the rain, and it looks like there's a storm setting in."

"Yes. I'm bushed as well. Do drive carefully, my love," she said and kissed him goodnight.

II

By midnight, the weather had gone from bad to worse. What started out as heavy rain had become a full-fledged storm with the wind howling through the trees, crashes of thunder and dazzling bolts of lightning illuminating the landscape with eerie flashes.

Rachel was having a nightmare. She dreamt she was covered in a black cloth and it was choking her. Although it felt smooth like silk, she couldn't breathe. She woke up with a start. The silk cover of the duvet was wrapped around her face, suffocating her. She untangled herself from it and sat up in bed. She could hear the wind howling outside and the pouring rain beating against her window panes. It was dark, and the fire had died down to a dim glow throwing dark shadows around the room that were lifted by intermittent flashes of lightening. That's when it struck her.

Of course! The black dress in the wardrobe! All crumpled up and thrown in next to the faded old bathrobe. It just didn't fit. Even the bedraggled bathrobe had been folded neatly. That was it. The tear on the dress had been superficial - nothing a good seamstress like Cindy couldn't fix. And yet, she had left it behind - in a crumpled heap. The same dress that she had lovingly bought material for, and spent hours making. Why was it left behind? It was cut in the latest fashion, and someone like Cindy could have worn it for several more occasions. There was something not right about it.

And then there was the picture of her in the dress. It was a lovely picture. Why did she leave it behind as well? *After all, there is nothing in the world that flatters the vanity of a woman than a well taken picture that captures and highlights her youth and beauty. Inevitably, women keep such pictures for posterity, with the silent hope in their hearts that future generations would gaze upon them in admiration and say, 'Our great-grandmother was a real beauty in her time!' What woman can resist keeping such a picture of herself. And yet Cindy had, for all intents and purposes, discarded it.*

And with the instinct of a woman, Rachel just knew. She knew that the memory of the day Cindy had worn the dress and had her picture taken must have been so painful or humiliating, that she wanted nothing more to do with either. *The same day that Cindy had possibly been the victim of a violent and possibly forced intercourse...*as the newspapers claimed. Had she been with Burt Hopworth? Mrs. Potter had called him the devil. What if there was someone else? Someone they hadn't even acknowledged yet as a suspect? *I must call Jeremy first thing in the morning.*

III

By early morning, the storm had passed but the sky was still overcast. Sleep had eluded Rachel, and she had tossed and turned through the remainder of the night, unable to get the smiling face of Cindy Jones out of her mind. The temperature had dropped a few degrees through the rainy night. It was chilly. She wrapped herself in her warmest robe and padded down the stairs in her fur-lined slippers to make a telephone call.

She met Betsy in the hall. She was carrying a tea tray up for someone.

"Why, Miss, you are up early. Would you like your morning tea now?" she asked, surprised to see Rachel up at that hour.

"Not now, Betsy, thank you. I must make an important call. And do come back soon. I need to ask you a few questions about Cindy," Rachel told her as she picked up the receiver of the telephone in the hall.

"Right, Miss, I'll just put the tea tray in Mrs. Holden's room and come back directly," Betsy said, looking rather curious.

"Hello. Yes operator. Get me 216 please," Rachel spoke into the telephone.

The phone bell seemed to ring interminably and was finally answered by a sleepy, muffled voice.

"Hello, 216. Who is this?" was the reply from the other end.

"Jeremy, this is Rachel. I need you to come over as soon as possible."

"My God Rachel, is everything alright? What's happened?" Jeremy asked. She could hear panic in his voice.

"Nobody's got killed last night, if that's what's got you worried, but I've realized that whoever Cindy met on the day she wore that dress is the killer. If it was Burt Hopworth, then we can rest easy. But what if it was someone else? We must find out who it was. And if the same person murdered Uncle Charles, we'll get him," she said jubilantly.

"What? What dress? Who didn't die in the night? You do realise you're not making any sense?" Jeremy asked, bewildered.

"Oh God! I can't explain over the telephone. You must come here, Jeremy. At once."

"Rachel, my darling, do you know what time it is?"

"It doesn't matter Jeremy. This is important. Don't you realise we'll crack this case wide open if we can just find out who had..."

"Sweetheart...stop please. Take a deep breath. I'm sure whatever this wonderful revelation is, it can wait till I wake myself up with some black coffee. Then after I've bathed and breakfasted, I shall see you. I'll be there by nine, I promise. Now goodbye."

She heard the click on the other end. The line went dead.

Five minutes later, Rachel cornered Betsy as she came downstairs.

"Betsy you helped Cindy stitch that black dress. You know, the one in the photograph."

"Yes Miss. I did the double stitch on the hem. Cindy was good with cutting out and stitching patterns, but she always asked me to do the hems on her special frocks. I'm good at that," Betsy said with some pride.

"Do you know if she was getting it ready for some special occasion? Like a dance somewhere? I mean, did she tell you when she was planning to wear it? Or who she was dressing up for?"

"Well, Miss, I can't be sure, but she did get asked out an awful lot. She could have worn it anywhere," Betsy replied.

"Oh, come on, Betsy! Do try and remember. Remember, the photograph was taken at some carnival. Can't you recall anything about it?" Rachel badgered her.

"I'm sure I'd tell you, Miss, if I remembered. But I just don't, Miss. What with all the work here at the hall, I only get a day off in a week, Miss. I 'ardly get to go out as much as Cindy could," Betsy replied, a little nervously. She could sense Rachel's impatience.

"I'm sorry, Betsy, for bullying you like this, but it's really important. Can you at least find out for me when this carnival thing was held and, if possible, who she went with?" Rachel asked her hopefully.

"Yes, Miss, but perhaps Sergeant Wilder can help you. They were more friendly like, and he may know more about this," Betsy answered.

"Oh, that's a good idea. Even if he doesn't know, he's sure to find it out for us. I'll ring the police station. Oh, but he wouldn't be there at this time, dash it! Does he have a telephone in his home?" Rachel asked, sounding distressed.

"That's not likely, Miss, but if you let me, I could go and bring him over. If I cut across the woods, I could be back in 'alf an hour. His house is in the village, not far from our end of the woods."

"Oh, would you Betsy? You are such a dear. I just want to get this sorted. Go quickly, and I'll inform Gladys that I've sent you out on an errand," Rachel said, heading towards the pantry to inform the cook and get herself a cup of tea.

Chapter Twenty Six

Rachel dressed warmly and awaited the arrival of Sergeant Wilder. It had been over half an hour, and there was still no sign of him or Betsy. She was getting impatient. Nobody was about, and since all the drapes around the house were still drawn, the house looked depressingly dark and gloomy. She decided to step outside and walk towards the woods.

It was cold, and the heavy rain had made the ground mushy. She had put on her wellingtons and taken an umbrella along, just in case the skies decided to open up again while she was out walking, but it didn't seem likely. The sky had brightened up a bit, and the air smelt crisp and clean. She could smell a wood fire burning somewhere in the distance. She felt invigorated. *This is great...I must get up early and go for walks more often,* she thought to herself.

Rachel had got as far as the summerhouse when she spotted Sergeant Wilder heading towards her. He greeted her with a wave from a distance, and she waved back.

"Good morning. What's all this I hear about you searching for the murderer, Miss Rachel? Betsy tells me you have an idea about who killed Miss Jones," he asked her as he reached her.

"Yes. You see, I've been doing my own bit of investigating and..."

"It's dangerous business, Miss. We'd rather you didn't get involved. Don't you think it's a better idea to leave it to the professionals? We don't want him coming after you now, do we?"

"Oh, but how could he? According to you all, he's locked up in a cell at the police station! Look, there's no point in heading back to the Hall. I'd rather we just step into the summerhouse and sit comfortably, away from prying eyes and ears, and I'll fill you in on my theory, which by the way, may not sound very sensible to you in the beginning but do hear me out. I'm quite sure I'm on the right track. You see, *I know how a woman's mind works!*"

"Alright, alright! I suppose it can't do us any harm," he said with a smile as they walked towards the glass doors of the summerhouse. He held it open and waved her in, "After you, Miss Rachel."

As they sat on the damp chairs in the summerhouse, Rachel told him everything, starting with her visit to Mrs. Potter, going through the girl's things, the sudden revelation in the middle of the night. He heard her out patiently. When she came to the end of her discourse, she looked at him expectantly.

He seemed uncomfortable. He finally spoke up, "That may be so, but nobody's going to take it seriously. Even if we find your mysterious Mr. X, you can't arrest anyone, leave alone convict them based on a half-baked theory of a discarded black dress! And heaven forbid, we even mention 'woman's intuition' in a case file! We'd be laughed out of court. Unless we can get a confession, which I frankly don't see happening."

"Yes, of course, I know all that! And I am not suggesting for a minute that we go up to this 'X' person and say, 'Hoy there, we know you did it...because she left her black dress behind! But don't you see, my idea is to point your minds towards someone you may not have even considered before. And think...I'm sure if the able police force decided to go about making the right enquiries – you know, interrogating this X's friends, neighbours or acquaintances, or even people who attended the carnival like the – stall keepers or fellow visitors, someone would've noticed something! You may well find some evidence in his house, if that's where he took her after the carnival forcibly. And then, who knows, we may even find a witness or two who will testify that they saw or heard him threatening her or heard her screams when he was hitting her. That ought to be enough to build up a case around him and then we've got him cornered. The idea is to make people think in a certain direction, towards a place where no one's mind has gone before. What if we've been barking up the wrong tree entirely? What if it wasn't Burt Hopworth after all? Once we find out who she was with, it may open up an entirely new line of investigation, and this time in the right direction!" Rachel said with complete conviction and gave him a determined nod.

"Very enlightening indeed. Have you shared your theory with anyone else yet, apart from what you told Betsy this morning?" he asked her casually.

"Well, yes and no. I tried to tell Detective Richards early this morning, but he was half asleep, and I don't think he understood a word I said. But why do you ask?"

"That's a relief." He shook his head. Then his voice changed "You think you are being rather clever, but you are, if I may say so, rather stupid. Going about, simply asking for trouble."

Something in his tone gave her an uneasy feeling. There was a long pause, and his next sentence chilled her.

"Cindy Jones was with me when she wore that black dress. I took her to the autumn carnival."

"Oh my God! It's you. It's been you all along. She was trying to escape from you. It was you she had a row with – the one Mrs. Potter overheard. You killed her. I should've known!" Rachel said, trying to stay calm. She realised no one knew she was here at the summerhouse with him. Not even Betsy. And it would take Jeremy another hour to get here... He had said he would arrive only by nine. By then, she would be dead. *I must stay calm. Keep him talking for some more time and then try and fight him off. But how? All I've got is a rickety old umbrella picked up from the hall stand.* The best bet would be to keep him talking for as long as possible...

"Well, it seems that once again, luck is on my side. Please don't get me wrong. I don't really want to kill you. If only you hadn't..." he said, as he got up and walked menacingly towards her.

"Look. Don't kill me... Well, I mean, not just yet. I'd haunt you for the rest of your life for an answer, if you did. I can't possibly die without knowing why you killed my uncle? Why?" Rachel pleaded.

"Why? Because the bastard deserved to die! Your uncle was the one who was planning to buy that farm in Kenya as an investment. He was waiting to hand over the money to Burt so that he could Charlie off to Africa and buy the farm on his behalf. He even offered him the job to stay back as an overseer. All that cock and bull story about Burt being offered a job by someone else."

"So that's what the money was for!"

"Yes. All I had planned to do was get to the money before Burt did. He told me that Sir Charles had told him that he could pick it up from the study table in case he was busy elsewhere...the old fool! He always had a soft corner for Burt..."

"But we were all under the impression that Burt was your closest friend. Where's your soft corner for him? How come you seem to hate him so much?"

"Hate him? I despise him. Ever since we were kids, all these fools always treated Burt differently... Just because he grew up at the fancy hall. For them all, he was always the better one, the charming one, getting the best of everything. The best girls, the most attention...he was the bloody apple of everybody's eye. I was the one who first noticed Cindy. I'm the one who had the courage to go upto her when we were seventeen. I'm the one she got friendly with first, but one smile from him and she goes off after him! She chose him. Over me! All I ever got were his discards. Always having to settle for second best. Even people like your uncle always gave him preferential treatment... Even after knowing he was rotten. Even after jail! But I knew, if the money went missing and Burt couldn't account for it, your dear old uncle would be the first person to put him behind bars again."

"That would've solved your problem. Why did you have to kill him?" Rachel asked.

"Because, like you, the old fool too, had bad timing. When I crept into the study to steal the money, he came back for something or other and caught me red handed. I had to kill him. I grabbed the first thing I saw and stabbed him, but he was a tough old man. He just wouldn't die. I finally had no other choice but to strangle him."

"How strenuous for you," Rachel commented acerbically.

"Okay, that's enough," Wilder bellowed.

"Wait! Wait...just one more question." Must *keep him talking. Jeremy or Betsy might just come looking for me.* "How did you find out Cindy was going to go with Burt? She was ever so careful about keeping it a secret."

"I knew Cindy was upto something and when Burt told me about Africa, I knew she'd go with him, the lousy bitch. All I had to do was reach the woods before Burt did. I knew she would be waiting for him there. I didn't even have to hunt her down. In the fog, she mistook me for him and came towards me. You should have seen the look on her face when she realised it was not Burt but me. I strangled her in no time."

"Charming!"

"Unlike the others, I think I'm going to enjoy killing you," he said, coming closer.

Rachel took a few steps back. She thought fast.

"Wait! I need to know why you killed her. Cindy. Why? You didn't love her. How would her leaving have made any difference to you?"

"How dare she push me away to go live with that idiot! She chose him over me! Over me! I wasn't about to let her get away. Oh, she played us both. She dumped him when he went to jail, and then she was all over me. She was the one who wanted to go to dances with me. I started taking her out more often. I damn near spent half my wages trying to show her a good time. And then, when I wanted something I knew she'd been giving Burt all along, for all the money I spent on taking her out, all the picture shows, all the fancy wining and dining, the tart turned on me. Said she *'didn't think of me that way.'*

"So you beat her and forced yourself on her? Ugh!"

"She got what she deserved. And she got it good. Getting me all hot and heavy and then trying to act all pure and innocent. She asked for it."

"I'm sure. The way I'm asking you to murder me, I suppose."

"You think you're very smart... Trying to buy more time, are we?"

"Sergeant Wilder, you can kill me, but you will hang. Betsy will tell everyone that I called for you and that you were the last person to see me alive, you know, unless you plan to bump her off too..." Rachel said, trying to keep the panic out of her voice.

"That will be unnecessary. All I have to do is go to the hall once I'm done with you here and presumably ask for you and wait to meet you. Nobody need know that we met here. Nobody will even suspect," he said in an ordinary, matter-of-fact voice that sent chills down her spine.

He was just a few feet away from her, and she realised her time had run out. She swung her umbrella with all the force she could muster and hit him over the head. He staggered. She took her chance and dashed towards the closed door, screaming at the top of her voice, "Help. Jeremy. Help. Betsy. Anybody. Help!" But he crossed the distance between them in two long strides and wrenched the umbrella out of her hand just as she took another swing. He threw the umbrella with such force that it shattered one of the glass panes of the summerhouse. The last thing she heard was the tinkling of glass, and then he hit her with the same force, and her world went black.

Chapter Twenty Seven

Rachel heard voices from afar..."Darling, open your eyes, please."Umm, Mother. There were more voices; all sounded familiar but she just wanted to go back into the lovely peaceful darkness. Then she heard a different voice, a man's voice...Jeremy, "Rachel, you can't do this to me. Come back to me, my darling or I'll never forgive myself." In her world, she smiled, but the delicious deep darkness was calling her. She wanted to float right back in to it and rest for a long, long time. For eternity. But that one voice wouldn't let her rest. Wouldn't let her go. It just kept getting louder. "Come back, my vixen. We have unfinished business. You have to come back. I'll give you no peace till you do, my girl. You have no choice but to come back to me. No Choice! Do you understand?" *No peace. No choice. Must turn back then. No choice...*

Slowly, the darkness gave way to light, and she found herself surfacing. Her eyes opened and she saw blurred faces around her.

"Oh, thank heavens! She's back."

II

A week later, the concussion that had almost killed her was healing well, and she was on the road to recovery. Rachel was still weak, but she could sit up on her bed, held up by cushions. Everyone had gathered in her room. She was surrounded by her family and, of course, Jeremy.

"I thought it was all over," Rachel announced weakly.

"We all did," Celia said.

"You gave us quite a scare," Major Markham said.

"If it hadn't been for Betsy's quick thinking, you probably wouldn't be here," Dennis said.

"I am never going to tick that girl off again for eavesdropping on conversations. It saved your life!" Lydia said.

Dennis spoke up, "And to think they damn near pinned the murders on me!"

"That was partly your stupidity, Dennis. Hiding Charles' body to save me as if I needed saving!" Celia said, as Dennis gave her a sheepish smile.

"Luckily for all, apart from Wilder actually being caught red handed attempting his third murder, they also found a thousand pounds of the stolen money stashed in his house. He planted most of it in Cindy Jones' belongings but couldn't resist keeping a nice little nest egg for himself. That cinched it!" Major Markham contributed.

"But something still puzzles me. Why was Burt still planning to sail to Africa without the money for the farm?" Rachel asked.

"According to him, he got cold feet. When he went to collect the money from the study as Charles had instructed him to do, he saw Celia running out with blood on her. He witnessed the accident. He knew there was trouble brewing and realised that if he stayed any longer, with his criminal record he was liable to be held responsible for whatever was going on at the hall. Anyway, he had the money for the passage and he thought he would wire his whereabouts to Charles once he reached Mombasa and, perhaps, something could be worked out. And money or no money, he was hell bent on boarding the ship to start a new life. Smart thinking on his part, I'd say. I'd have done the same thing if I were in his shoes!" Major Markham said.

At this point, Hopworth, the butler, Betsy and Suzie entered with two large tea trays and another tray stacked with plates and cutlery. As they set up the tea in the room, Hopworth spoke to Rachel.

"Good afternoon, Miss Rachel. My wife and I are deeply indebted to you for saving our son Burt. I shudder to think, Miss, what they would have done to him if it wasn't for you and Mr. Richards here."

Rachel spoke, "Oh Hopworth. You must've realised by now, that he is a good boy. I do hope you've sorted out your differences. If this terrible episode has taught us anything, it would be that life is unpredictable. Life is too short, I think, to be separated from the ones that we love, don't you agree?"

"Yes, Miss Rachel. And everyone has been so kind to us and to him. Burt has changed his mind about going to Africa. He will be staying here at the hall with us. Lady Celia has offered him the post of Estate Manager for Rutherford Hall," Hopworth said, his eyes shining with pride.

Celia addressed Rachel, "Yes, now with Charles gone, your father and I have decided that we can use Burt's education and his knowledge about the estate, given that he grew up here, to help us with estate accounts and running the estate in general." Then turning towards Hopworth, she said gently, "Charles had a touching faith in your boy, Hopworth, and he wanted to help him. I'm sure he would have liked it this way."

Hopworth replied, "I am to no end grateful to Lord Rutherford, God rest his soul. And to you all. I wish I had shown as much faith in my boy, Madam, as you all have..." he left off, his voice faltering with uncharacteristic emotion. He put his mind to setting out the tables, but his hand was shaking. The parlourmaids threw glances in his direction as they handed out cups of tea and served the sandwiches and tea cakes around. They had never seen him so close to tears before.

Rachel smiled and decided to change the topic to make things a little less awkward for Hopworth.

"Will someone please tell me how I managed to evade being body number three? I've just been dying to know, and nobody's told me anything about that," Rachel asked plaintively.

Jeremy spoke. "It's quite simple, really. Betsy had gone to Sergeant Wilder's house and told him what you had told her and that you wanted him to come over to the hall. She said he looked angry, but she thought it was probably because the detour to the hall would spoil his morning routine. Then, after she left Wilder's house, she decided she would go and have a word with Mrs. Potter and tell her about your theory. She did. Mrs. Potter informed her that Cindy had gone out with Sergeant Wilder the day she had worn the black dress. Don't ask me how, but Betsy knew you were in danger. She wasn't unduly alarmed as she knew he couldn't harm you up at the hall. But again, she wasn't too sure. She and Mrs. Potter discussed it, and they both decided the safest thing would be to go to a telephone box and call you to warn you. But when Hopworth said you weren't in the house and that he hadn't seen Wilder either, they got worried, and then Betsy did a smart thing. She remembered my number from earlier that morning when she overheard you calling me, and she called me and told me everything. I drove like hell. On reaching the hall, the first thing I did was head towards the woods thinking he may have dragged you there but before I could reach the woods, I heard you scream for help and then the sound of glass shattering, and I knew he had you in the summerhouse. I reached you just in time, not a moment too soon, and saw him strangling you. After that, I just saw red. The rest, as they say, is history."

"Well, I'm glad I'm not history. Thank you Betsy!" she said.

Betsy acknowledged her role in the events that had transpired with a shy smile and a soft spoken, "You are welcome, Miss Rachel. And I am very glad that Mr. Jeremy got here in time, Miss."

Rachel spoke, "Yes Betsy, you are quite right. I must not forget to thank Jeremy for saving my life, among other things," she said, looking lovingly at him. She held out her hand to him, and he came over and kissed her on the forehead. Then he pulled up a chair from the corner and sat by her bedside holding her hand.

The tea service completed, Hopworth and the parlourmaids took their leave.

Major Markham spoke, "You'll be happy to know, my dear, that Jeremy quite nearly made Wilder, body number three. Luckily, Betsy had rushed back to the hall and Hopworth had raised the alarm. I reached just in time to prevent him from finishing off Wilder completely. So now, there's something leftover for the hangman to hang," he said, taking a bite out of the cucumber sandwich Gladys had provided.

"Yes, that's good to know. But this entire week I've been cooped up here on my own hasn't been a total loss. I've had plenty of time to think and, I've made up my mind to marry Jeremy," Rachel announced.

"My dear!" Elizabeth exclaimed. "It's the concussion speaking. You can't be serious."

"Mother, I've never been more serious about anything in my life. Jeremy, will you marry me? In front of my entire family, I solemnly promise that I'll try not to nag you too much, and more importantly, I promise to never ever cook for you," Rachel said, smiling at him.

Jeremy responded with a smile, "My darling, who can refuse a proposal of such romantic magnitude? I thought I'd wait till you get better to pop the question myself. I went mad when I thought I was going to lose you. But as in all other things, you've beaten me to it, my beautiful, smart woman. But I want to ask you again – Are you sure you want marriage, that too with a grouchy old bachelor like me? Are you quite sure?"

Rachel nodded happily.

"In that case, I suppose I have no choice in the matter. Lady Elizabeth and Major Markham, despite your strong views regarding age differences in a marriage, I'm afraid I am going to have to accept your daughter's proposal. Think of it this way, you are not losing a daughter but you are gaining a son-in-law. Congratulations!"

Epilogue

SIX MONTHS LATER...

Jeremy and Rachel had a lovely late April wedding at the tiny church on the hill. Golden sunshine streamed down through the antique stained glass windows and gave a jewelled effect to the ceremony. All those who attended felt they had never seen a more radiant bride as she walked down the flower-laden aisle on her father's arm.

After the wedding, there had been a feast to remember at Rutherford Hall. Practically the entire village had shown up to bless the union of their favourite heroes, for by now it was widely acknowledged that Rachel and Jeremy had worked in tandem with the police to catch the ruthless killer, who had ironically given the sleepy little village its own aura of notoriety and a spot on England's map of noteworthy places.

Meanwhile, Celia had made her peace with Charles' death, and had worked closely with Dennis to complete *and publish Lord Rutherford's memoirs, which included a transcript of the events that had swept the imagination of the whole country. It was a best seller. A week later, while Rachel's wedding preparations were in full swing at the hall, Dennis had gone down on one knee and given voice to the topmost desire in his heart... That he had no other wish but to spend the rest of his days with Celia by his side. To his great joy, she said yes and they were to be married in September. They planned to visit India for their honeymoon. Dennis had a silent hope that, on this visit, he would find the ideal tea plantation to gift his wife, one they could revisit every summer.*

Lydia Holden continued to live at the hall but with her new found respect for the staff, she chose to turn her immense energy towards teaching at the local Sunday School and joining the Women's Institute. The past Wednesday, her lecture on 'A Woman's Role in British India' had been full of interesting snippets from her life in India, and she had received a standing ovation. She had started making new friends in the village, who prompted her to help organise the church fete held in March! The general consensus had been that she was one of the best organisers the village had ever had. She had finally found her forte.

Celia had requested that Lady Elizabeth and James Markham consider making Rutherford Hall their permanent home. She couldn't imagine living there with just Dennis and her mother for company. After all, a large house like Rutherford needed a large family to bring its rooms to life. Lady Elizabeth gave her offer some consideration and finally agreed that it would be a good idea for both parties to live together in the family home, on the condition, that they be allowed to contribute in equal parts towards running expenses.

Lady Elizabeth had come into a comfortable inheritance left to her by her brother and had decided wisely to control it herself, by investing in the same gilt-edged securities her brother had preferred. Major Markham continued to approach her with wildcat schemes from time to time, only to be turned down flatly and finally made his peace with it, since each time, people who had invested in them, unfailingly lost all their money. For that, he was grateful that his wife held the purse strings.But his eyes would still light up if someone mentioned an impossible return on a railroad scheme somewhere in South America.

Burt settled down at Rutherford Hall and, with the reassurance of his father's guidance, he flourished as an estate manager. During the course of his duties, he had met and fallen in love with the local veterinarian's daughter, and they were 'steppin' out' together, as his proud mother Gladys liked to say.

Inspector Parker kept in touch with Jeremy and Rachel, and from time to time, they would invite the inspector over for dinner at Sunny Ridge, as they had the night before. The discussion had touched upon various topics but came to rest finally on an interesting case in Devon where a family of six had lost two of its members to mysterious deaths. The police were baffled. And George Mayer, the Superintendent of Police, had requested Inspector Parker's help in the case, owing to his recent success in the Rutherford murder case.

After the inspector had bid them goodbye, Rachel ventured, "Do you know, Jeremy, I think we could do with a refreshing seaside holiday. Think...lovely clotted cream and going bathing in the sea. Hmm."

"Why am I getting the feeling that your sudden need for dairy products and a dip in the sea, is just a ruse to take me along on another madcap murderous hunt?" he asked her suspiciously, his eyes narrowing into slits.

"Oh, please, darling. Just this once. Think how helpful we can be to poor Inspector Parker. I mean, seriously, without our help, I wonder if he would've even remotely suspected that the killer had been his very own personal sidekick all along! He so needs our help," she said as she turned to him, her eyes shining with possibility.

And Jeremy found himself groaning out loud, "Oh no! Not again!"

Murder at Ravenrock

A Rachel Markham Mystery

Book Two – In the Mystery Series

Sofia Burnett, the beautiful American actress, married to the British millionaire - Henry Cavendish, spoke up, as if coming out of a daze, "My God! There really is a lunatic about. And from the looks of it, he's trying to wipe out the family, up at Ravenrock, one by one."

When a spate of baffling murders, rock the charming albeit sleepy town of Dartmouth, in Devon, Rachel and Jeremy, must go all out, to unravel the mysterious deaths, and unmask the ingenious criminal mind behind them.

Set in 1947, England, Murder at Ravenrock is an intriguing sequel to PB Kolleri's first book, 'Murder at Rutherford Hall.'

Made in the USA
Lexington, KY
01 February 2014